Asher

Tiffany Casper

Zagan MC

Book 1

Copyright © Tiffany Casper 2024

All rights reserved. No part of this publication may be reproduced, distributed, or transmitted in any form or by any means, including photocopying, recording, or other electronic or mechanical methods, without the prior written permission of the publisher, except in the case of brief quotations embodied in critical reviews and certain other noncommercial uses permitted by copyright law.

Any references to historical events, real people, or real places are used fictitiously. Names, characters, and places are products of the author's imagination.

Acknowledgments

To all my readers who have become a part of the Wrath Family, I thank you!!!

The Wrath Family is all-encompassing, you never have to feel as though you are alone.

And if you feel like you are, shoot me a message, and I will remind you that you are not.

– Tiffany.

Synopsis

Chloe

The saying that everything happens for a reason couldn't be further from the truth.

Had I known when I stood up to a bully, I would have gotten to claim the best person I know as my best friend... I wouldn't have changed a single thing.

Even more so when that put me in sight of her dad.

And being in those sights for well over half my life, it does something to a person.

It makes you realize that when he claimed your heart at just nine years old, you later found out that you wouldn't be getting it back.

And you didn't want it back.

You wanted him to keep it forever and keep it safe.

But little would you know that things aren't always as they appear.

And sometimes, you must be okay with everything, not being black and white but adding gray to the mix.

Asher

Being the president of a one percenter motorcycle club was the only dream I went after and got it.

Being Stella's dad was the most important thing in my life.

But had I known all of that would change when I started noticing things about her when she turned sixteen... I wouldn't have done anything differently.

But one.

Even after all the things I've done. All the lives I've taken.

Hurting her has been my one regret.

And I will be damned if I don't fix it and finally claim the one person who is my soul's other half.

HEA/No Cheating/Age-Gap/Best Friend's Dad

Zagan MC

Asher – President

Whit – Vice President

Priest – Enforcer

Creature – Enforcer

Rome – SGT at Arms

Pipe – Secretary

Irish – Road Captain

Trigger – Treasurer

Charlie – Tech

Coal – Icer

Playlist

Ain't No Rest for the Wicked – Cage the Elephant

Just Like Fire – P!nk

In Your Love – Tyler Childers

She Never Lets It Go To Her Heart – Tim McGraw

Let Her Go – Passenger

Can't You See – The Marshall Tucker Band

To Make You Feel My Love – Garth Brooks

Table of Contents

Asher

Copyright © Tiffany Casper 2024

Acknowledgments

Synopsis

Zagan MC

Playlist

Table of Contents

Prologue

Chapter 1

Chapter 2

Chapter 3

Chapter 4

Chapter 5

Chapter 6

Chapter 7

Chapter 8

Chapter 9

Chapter 10

Chapter 11

Chapter 12

Chapter 13

Chapter 14

Chapter 15

Chapter 16

Chapter 17

Chapter 18

Chapter 19

Epilogue

Thank You

Stalk Me

Other Works

Prologue

Asher

They say that everything in your life can change in just one second.

One tick in time in this big clock wheel we all live in.

And if you don't believe it, you haven't spent hours thinking about it.

And if you don't believe it, you need to open your eyes.

Because that has happened to me quite a few times. Thirteen of them, to be exact.

The first time I saw a man drive by the single-wide trailer, we lived in on a motorcycle. He hadn't been wearing a helmet, his long blonde hair was flying behind him. And there, at that moment, I told myself that I would buy a bike and drive it, which was why, at fifteen, I bought my first one by doing odd jobs here and there.

The second time, I had a revelation of sorts. I can't tell you how the thought came to me, but it had. I had met a man named Stoney and Whit. From there, we formed Zagan MC.

The third time, a woman I had fucked came to me months after and told me she was pregnant. I wasn't a fool, mind you, even though I was young, you can bet your ass I had a DNA test done.

The baby was mine.

The fourth, I held my daughter for the first time. I don't recall the woman's eyes who had placed my daughter in my arms. But I do recall the very first time I looked into my daughter's face. She was a mini replica of me. And up until that point, I had never seen anything more beautiful.

The fifth time, well, I would get to that later in the story. There's a person I need to tell all that to.

The sixth time was when I laid eyes on a young girl. And that time, well, that was when I hadn't realized my entire life had changed in that one split second as she climbed out of her mother's car.

The seventh time, well, that was when I realized my life had changed on that fateful day all those years later. And it was also when I realized I needed to have my head examined.

Because any man who is a man at all doesn't check out a girl that isn't legal.

But alas, I am a man. And we are stupid. We are assholes. We are dicks.

And we keep being assholes, dicks, shitheads, all the things, but we just hope and pray that the ones we love will keep all those things in mind when they outweigh the pros and cons of dealing with our sorry asses.

Which leads me to the eighth, ninth, tenth, eleventh, twelfth, and the thirteenth time my life changed in a second. And every single one of those, with the exception of one, involves one certain woman.

I thought that the greatest fear any man could ever have was having something that was the owner of their heart walking around in a world and being vulnerable.

But no. That's not the greatest fear any man could ever have.

The greatest fear, in my opinion, is fucking something up and knowing without a shadow of a doubt that if you don't repair and fix what you broke, well, then you might as well accept the fact that you will be a shell of your former self.

And all you will want is for the maker to call your sorry ass home.

See? Men can be stupid, assholes, dickheads, shitheads, you name it, we can definitely be it.

That is how my story is going to start.

But first, I want you to get to know how it all came to be.

That way, when you get to our story, you won't think I'm a fucking creeper.

Chapter 1

Chloe – Past – Age 15

"Okay, now where is the party at again?" My mama asked.

"It's at Stella's house," I told her as I packed my bag.

Stella wanted a slumber party at her house instead of doing it at the clubhouse.

A clubhouse I had been way too many times to count.

I loved it there.

It was awesome.

None of the kids at school could say they had seen the inside of it.

But Stella and I could.

Stella because her daddy was the president of Zagan MC.

I learned during a crash course when we were nine years old what all the patches on their kuttes were called and what they meant.

And that black patch with the 1% logo on it in white thread meant they didn't obey the law. They had their own.

And I also learned that Zagan MC's only laws were these.

Never betray a brother.

Never hurt family.

Never hurt women or kids.

And no drugs. Except for pot because it didn't make a lick of sense why it was illegal.

And that was it.

Those were the rules in Zagan MC.

Mr. Hendrix, Stella's dad, had started the MC when he was eighteen years old.

I still didn't know why he had created the club, but maybe one day I would find out about it.

I also learned that things on the show *Sons of Anarchy* didn't portray an actual club all that well. But some of the actors were nice to look at.

But I was able to compare the officers of the club.

See, you had Mr. Hendrix; Asher was the president.

Whit was the vice president. I swore I often wonder why his road name isn't something like Viking. Because he looks like a Norse god. Right down to the long braid, his hair was always in, and the blonde hair and blue eyes.

Rome was the sergeant at arms. He was almost considered a mute. He only talked when he wanted to. And when he did talk, you freaking listened to him.

Irish was the road captain, and it was funny as all get out when we sometimes battled with our tempers.

The secretary position was open, but they hadn't found anyone to fill it. I also learned that they were waiting for a brother who had been a nomad for the longest time to come back. And they were keeping the position open for him.

Trigger was the treasurer and a crack shot. It was awesome watching him use his skills at the target practice area the MC had set up.

Ox was just a member. But he had been with Asher when he started the club. I didn't know much about him.

Stoney didn't have an official title or anything.

He had just been a man who had gone through life and was tired of the bureaucratic BS, his words.

Coal was the icer for the club. I knew that Wrath MC, Soulless Outlaws, Pagans Soldiers, and Immoral Saints all had that term. But no other clubs did.

I didn't know what the Icer did, and neither did Stella and the time we brought it up to her dad, he simply told us that he would explain that term when we were both eighteen.

Priest was the enforcer for the club, and he was a beast.

But he was nothing compared to Creature.

And Creature. You had to take Beast from *Beauty and the Beast* and have him make a kid with the most scarred-up individual you've ever met.

That was Creature. If Rome was almost considered a mute, then Creature was a mute. He didn't speak to anyone. That perhaps had something to do with the damage he received to his vocal cords. But I didn't know about his story.

I was taken out of my thoughts when my mama asked me, "Who all is going to be there?"

Before I could answer my mama, my daddy came up the stairs and asked, "Is she ready?"

I smiled at him when I saw him and then answered my mama.

"Our friends, Casey, Nora, Poppy, Lizzie, and Maria, are going to be there. And the brothers of Zagan MC."

"And what about a female figure?" Mama asked.

"Priest's wife is going to be there," I told her.

Since she had met all of them, she nodded, "Okay. If you need anything, I want you to call us. Okay?"

I nodded. "Okay, Mama."

And with that, I finished packing my little duffle bag for the hamburgers and hotdogs and the slumber party, and then I grabbed Stella's present.

We all went down the stairs when there was a knock on the door.

My mama looked at my daddy and asked, "Are you expecting anyone?"

My daddy shook his head, "No. You?"

And when my mama shook her head, my daddy moved to open the door.

Laughing when he saw who it was.

It was one of my daddy's oldest friends, Marco Rubina.

That man creeped me out.

I couldn't put a finger on it.

But it was something.

I watched as my daddy shook his hand and gestured for him into the house.

My mama placed her hand on my shoulder.

Could she feel the creepiness rolling off him in waves like I could?

And he further proved the creepiness when his eyes swept over my body, and I swore I saw something flicker in his eyes before it was gone.

Thankfully, my mama squeezed my shoulder and led me out to her car.

As we were headed to Stella's house, I asked, "Does Marco feel weird to you?"

She looked at me from the corner of her eye and shrugged, "That's just Marco. He's a good man."

I nodded, then tried to remove him from my thoughts.

In twenty minutes, we were pulling up in front of Stella's house.

Her house sat on ten acres of land, and it was one of those old Victorian-style houses, and sometimes I envisioned that I lived there.

I really wanted to turn the nook that overlooked the driveway into a reading corner.

It would be awesome.

And it needed a bright purple wingback chair to read it.

The front door opened, and Stella ran out, "You're here. You're here."

I giggled, then leaned over and kissed my mama's cheek, "Love you, Mama."

She smiled, "Love you too, Mija. Have a fun time."

Once I was out of the car, my bag and Stella's gift in my hand, we walked arm-in-arm up to her house.

Her dad, Mr. Hendrix, stood in the open doorway, then he took my bag and her gift and said, "Y'all go have fun."

I smiled, "Thanks, Mr. Hendrix."

He groaned. "You're making me feel old, Chloe. Why can't you call me Asher?"

I giggled up at him, "Because it's disrespectful, and my mama would wash my mouth out with soap."

He chuckled and then closed the door as we walked into the house.

***

The party was in full swing.

The girls and I sat in a circle, making crowns out of daisy chains while rock music played in the background.

And since *AC/DC* was her favorite band, they played nothing but that music.

Which was why I was singing along to the lyrics, way out of tune, but that was okay.

So, look at me now, I'm just makin' my play. Don't try to push your luck, just get out of my way.

Stella grinned at me, and together we sang the lyrics.

After we all had all the crowns on, Poppy said, "Do y'all want to play a game my older sister plays with her friends?"

We all shrugged and then nodded.

Poppy said, "Okay, so it goes like this. You must name someone you would kiss, date, and then marry. And it must be actors or actresses."

"Since Stella is the birthday girl, she gets to go first." Maria giggled.

We all looked at Stella as she tilted her head and thought for a moment, and then she said, "Kiss, it would have to be Jensen. Date, it would be Jared. Something about those *Supernatural* boys. Marry, it would totally have to be Jason Momoa."

We all giggled.

"It's that long hair?" Casey asked.

"You are too right," Stella said as she laughed.

Maria went next, "Kiss, it would have to be Charlie Hunnam. To date, it would have to be Freddie Prince Jr. And to marry, hmm, I guess I will have to go with David Beckham."

"You are all over the place," Casey snickered.

Maria shrugged, "I like the variety. Sue me."

Casey chuckled, "Okay, I'll go next. To kiss, I will go with Josh Hartnett. To date, definitely Ben Affleck. And to marry, I gotta go with Ewen Bremner."

I snickered; Casey had a thing for the movie *Pearl Harbor*.

Nora giggled, "Okay, I have to go with Glen Powell to kiss. To date, I have to pick Josh Duhamel. And to marry, I definitely have to go with Scott Eastwood."

Poppy laughed, "Dang. Those are my choices, too. But to kiss, it has to be Jason Momoa."

Lizzie chuckled, "What is it about Jason Momoa, I just don't get it."

Stella and Poppy chimed in then, "The tattoos. The Muscles. The hair." And then they both fist-bumped each other.

And then it was my turn. I had been thinking about this and knew my answer.

They all looked at me, and I sighed, "I guess I'm going to be different. I pick Jensen Ackles for all three."

They laughed while Maria giggled, "You gotta pick three different men."

I shrugged, "I can't. I don't know. I guess I'm a one-man kind of girl."

Stella grinned at me, "There's nothing wrong with that."

Lizzie smiled, "Stella's right. You just do you, girl. It's working."

"What are y'all over here giggling about?" Mr. Hendrix asked.

Maria giggled, "Nothing, Mr. Hendrix."

Poppy nodded, "Yeah, you know, just girl talk."

Stella smiled up at her dad, "Just girl talk, Daddy."

Then he looked at me, and me being me, I said, "No comment."

That caused everything to snicker and then burst out with laughter.

It was after we ate burgers and hot dogs, had a dance party, and had cake that I was at the kitchen sink when I caught Mr. Hendrix walking into the kitchen.

"Wanna tell me what y'all were talking about?" Mr. Hendrix asked as I finished washing my hands.

I looked up at him and smiled, "No comment."

He groaned, "Damn. Okay, well, do I have anything to worry about when it comes to my girl?"

I giggled, "No. But even if you did, as long as it wouldn't put her in danger, I still wouldn't tell you."

That was when he gestured to the kutte that hung over his body, "You realize you're telling the president of an outlaw club, no. Right?"

I giggled again, I couldn't help it, "Yes, I realize that. But to me, you're not in an outlaw club. Nor are you a president. You're Stella's dad."

The moment the last word fell from my mouth, Stella called out, "Chloe, did we do *Transformers* last year?"

I smiled, then called out, "Yeah. And if you will wait to open your gift, you'll know what you're getting."

I looked up at Mr. Hendrix and said, "Five. Four. Three. Two. One."

And just like that, she came racing into the kitchen, skidding on her socks, gasping, "You didn't?"

I mockingly gasped, "I didn't do what?"

Stella jerked her head up to her dad, "Can we open presents now?"

He chuckled, then ruffled her hair, "Yeah, Princess. Yeah."

Once everyone gathered in the living room, presents were exchanged.

This was my favorite part about giving gifts to people, seeing their smiles.

Stella's gasp and then the dreamy look at her new present from me had me giggling.

She would be able to get her something about those *Supernatural* boys fix anytime she wanted to.

I felt eyes on the side of my face, but I didn't dare turn it.

It didn't hit me until I closed my eyes that night in the living room that Stella's dad hadn't asked any of our friends to call him Asher but me. That was weird.

Chapter 2

Asher – Past – Age 37

Two weeks before Stella's sweet sixteen party, I had an idea.

And to do this idea, I had to somehow get Chloe alone for a minute.

Thankfully, I managed that when they were at the clubhouse doing their homework.

Stella had run to the kitchen to get something to eat.

I sat down beside Chloe, who looked at me and smiled, and then said, "Hey, Mr. Hendrix."

Somehow.

Some way, I was going to get her to stop calling me that shit. It made me feel older than dirt.

But now wasn't the time.

I had to do this before Stella came back.

I lowered my tone and said, "Need you to do me a favor?"

She looked at me, tilted her head to the side, and said, "Umm, okay."

"Need you to go with Stella to this." I told her and showed her the tickets I got for Stella.

It was the first part of her birthday present.

I'd already talked to Chloe's parents, and they had been fine with it.

It was two tickets to Comic-Con, and the actors who played in Supernatural were going to be there.

Chloe saw what it was and knew, then she groaned, "Seriously? You know how much squealing she's going to do. Do you want my ears to bleed?"

I snickered, "She's your best friend, Chloe."

She sighed, "Fine. I'll do it. But you so owe me."

I nodded, "Anytime you want to cash in your marker, you just let me know," I told her.

Just then, I heard, "What's going on?"

Chloe looked up at Stella and grinned, "Did you know your dad is super smart?"

Stella nodded skeptically, "Yeah. Why?"

"Because I couldn't figure out this fraction. He showed me how." Lying through her teeth for me. Then she looked at me, nodded, and said, "Thanks, Mr. Hendrix."

I nodded, "Any time."

Then I stood up and walked away.

Wondering how in the world anyone could tell when Chloe was lying.

But I had a feeling that she didn't do it that often.

And when she did, she told the truth afterward.

Which was what she did when she showed up at my house to go with Stella.

***

I chuckled when Stella ran to her car.

Today was Stella's sweet sixteen birthday.

We had the party at the house since she wanted to invite some friends from school who didn't need to be around the clubhouse.

The light blue Volkswagen Beetle with a soft black top was her dream car.

I didn't get it.

But then again, I wasn't a girl.

Chloe was hot on her heels, hugging her and taking pictures of her as she posed this way and that way.

"Anyone ever tells you you're a bad father, tell them to shove it where the sun doesn't shine," Stoney chimed in at my side.

I chuckled, then nodded, "Yeah."

Once her big present was revealed and the food was eaten, we gathered around the fire in the backyard, beers to those who could drink it and sparkling apple cider to those who couldn't.

And just like always, which never seemed to fail, even if we didn't plan that shit, I was sitting beside Chloe, and Stella was on her other side.

Suddenly, Stella jumped up and then raced into the house.

I lifted a brow and then looked at Chloe, who was laughing her ass off.

"What the fuck is so funny?" I asked her once she stopped laughing.

She snickered, "She's been holding her bladder for seven hours now. She thought it would be funny to chug that last cider."

I chuckled at my girl. Only Stella.

Then I sighed and brought something up that we seemed to bicker about, "What is it going to take for you to call me Asher?" I asked.

Chloe shrugged, "I don't know."

I took a pull from my beer and then said, "I don't think it's disrespectful."

She shrugged again.

"What if you called me something else that only you called me? Would that help?" I asked.

She lifted her head, "Like what?"

Fuck, if I knew. Hell, she could call me dickhead or asshole. I was just tired of the Mr. Hendrix shit. But then, one name came to mind, "Ash?"

She wrinkled her nose, "No way. That's a girl's nickname. And you are definitely not a girl."

I had to bite back the words along the lines of, *glad you noticed.*

Because I didn't know where the hell that thought came from.

Thankfully before any more could be said and I creeped myself out and crossed lines that didn't make any fucking sense to me, Stella came back and asked, "What are you two talking about?"

Chloe sighed, "Your dad is getting fed up with me being respectful and calling him Mr. Hendrix."

Stella snickered, "I'm surprised he's put up with it for this long."

Chloe shrugged, "I can't help that I was raised with manners."

Stella placed her hands on her hips, "Are you saying I was raised in a barn?"

Chloe snickered, "If the shoe fits."

I chuckled at her answer, and then she looked at me, then at Stella, and sighed.

Then she looked back at me, "You're not going to give in to this, are you?"

I shook my head slowly, "No, ma'am."

She sighed, "Fine. I'll stop calling your Mr. Hendrix, and I'll call you Pres."

I felt something in my gut tighten.

What the fuck was that about?

That would have been perfectly acceptable.

But before I could put words to my thoughts, my mouth said, "No. Doesn't seem right either. You're not a brother. It's Asher or nothing else."

She sighed.

Then, in an exasperated way, she rolled her eyes and said, "Fine. Asher."

And the moment I heard my name fall from her lips, I had to pretend I got a call and then walked away like I had the hounds of hell on my heels.

She's sixteen.

She's my daughter's best friend.

What the fuck had I been thinking?

Mr. Hendrix was fine.

But... the way my name sounded in her husky voice.

Holy. Shit.

Chapter 3

Chloe – Past – Age 17

"Okay, what about him?" Stella tilted her head to the corner of the cafeteria.

I looked in that direction, then I looked back at her and said, "Not my type."

She groaned, "Come on, Co. Someone at this school has to be your type."

I shook my head at her, "I'm sorry, Stell."

She sighed, "I would do it for you."

And she would.

But I just wasn't like that, and she knew it.

I gave her the best apologetic eye look I could muster, then said, "I'm sorry, Stell. I just can't make something happen if I don't feel it."

She sighed again, "I know. And it's one of the things I love about you."

I grinned, "Tell you what, when I find someone who makes my heart beat double time, you'll be the first to know. Okay?"

Inwardly, I cringed.

Because I couldn't tell her who made my heart beat double time. Who caused my breath to stall in my lungs when I spoke to him. Who caused every single nerve ending in my body to fire.

But thankfully, Stella couldn't read any of that on my face.

And I knew that when she smiled and nodded, "Okay. You better."

Just then, Poppy, Casey, Nora, Maria, and Lizzie made it to our table.

They sat their lunch trays down, and Nora lowered her voice, "Word in the halls is that Brett and Karla finally called it quits for good."

We didn't gasp.

We didn't snicker.

No, we busted out laughing.

Because they were on and off again so many times that it was insane.

I swear that they broke up more times than I changed my underwear.

"What's everyone saying?" Poppy asked as she took a bite of her pizza.

Nora shrugged, "Well, the word is that Brett has been trying to end things with her because there's someone else he's really into. And he didn't want her to get caught up in their drama. Supposedly, she doesn't deserve that, and she's too good for that."

Poppy swooned, "Aww. That's sweet."

Maria looked at Poppy, winked at her, and then asked, "Any idea who that girl is?"

Nora shook her head, "Nope. No clue. But we do know that she goes here."

Everyone gasped but me.

I really didn't get all that drama that surrounded Brett.

Sure. He was good-looking in that GQ kind of way. The football god of the school.

Brett was a little over six feet with blue eyes and dirty blonde hair. He was fit.

I got the allure of it all, but for me, he just didn't tick the right boxes.

He wasn't taller. He didn't have the right color of hair. His eyes didn't make me melt.

He didn't stand next to me and make me feel so small but so protected at the same exact time.

Thankfully, Lizzie started talking about what she was planning to do this weekend.

And that steered the conversation away from Brett and who the mystery girl could possibly be.

However, it wasn't long before a few names were thrown around about who the girl could be.

Once we went back to our classes, I settled in my seat in calculus beside Stella and opened my textbook.

I was reviewing a few things when I saw a shadow fall over me.

Lifting my head, it was to see Brett.

The topic of our lunch period.

And the topic of the entire school, apparently.

He winked, "How's it going, Chloe?"

I lifted a brow, "Fine. What are you doing in here?"

He smirked, "You're in here. That's why."

I didn't say anything.

Because what was there to say?

I saw something on his face change.

Was that... shock?

But before I could really process that look, it was gone. Then he said, "I got a question for you."

I shrugged, even though I was getting uncomfortable because I could feel a lot of eyes on us, and I needed this to be done with, whatever this was. I said, "Shoot."

"There's this new pizza place they just opened on Main Street. You and me, Friday night?"

I shook my head, "Thanks. But I've got plans."

And with that, I looked back down at my textbook.

And from the corner of my eye, I saw Stella's mouth hanging wide open, and then she closed it and hissed, "Our plans aren't that important. Say yes."

I looked over at her, "No. We have plans. I would be the world's crappiest friend if I canceled our plans for some guy."

"Admire that." I heard from Brett.

I sighed, then looked up at him, "Frankly, I don't care."

He chuckled, "You got sass. I fucking like that. Saturday?"

I shook my head, "Plans then too."

Stella once again hissed, "We have parties every weekend, it won't hurt you to miss one."

Brett chuckled, "I like you. What's your name?"

I saw Stella's frame soften, and then she whispered, "Stella."

He jerked up his chin, "Cool to meet you." Then he looked back at me, "Saturday. Give me your phone."

I didn't move except to lean back in my chair and cross my arms over my chest, "I. Have. Plans. Now, you are holding up this class. If you wouldn't mind leaving... I'd appreciate that."

He rocked back on his heels, tongued his cheek, then looked behind me and said, "Move."

I almost lost my stuffing.

What I wouldn't give to say, I almost lost my shit.

But if my mama ever heard me say a curse word... I cringed.

There were a few things that scared me. But disappointing my mama was the biggest one of them all.

The guy behind me scampered out of his chair and moved to a different one.

The moment the guy moved, Brett slid into the chair.

I rolled my eyes, and then, all through class, I ignored Brett.

The moment the bell rang, I got out of my chair and looked at him, "I thought telling you I had plans would clue you in, but apparently, I'm going to have to be blunt. I'm not interested."

With that, I grabbed my stuff and then headed out of class, Stella was on my heels the entire way, and the moment we hit the hall that would separate us for our last class of the day, she said, "Come on sugar pumpkin. Munchkin kisses forever and ever. Say yes to him. He's the god of this school."

"I wouldn't go that far, but I'd like to change your mind and make you interested in me," Brett said from our side.

I threw my hands up and then stomped away.

All the while, I heard Brett chuckle at my back.

Once classes were over for the day, I made my way to Stella's light-blue Volkswagen beetle convertible.

Just as I made it to the door, I saw her running.

"I'm going to talk you into going out with him even if it kills me," she said, huffing.

I snickered, "Fat chance. But good luck trying."

And on the way to the clubhouse, where we always went after school so we could get homework done, our chat group started blowing up.

After I read the first one from Nora, I silenced my phone.

Nora – *Brett asked you out. And you told him you had plans??? WTF??? SMH!!!!*

Once we made it to the clubhouse, I was five seconds away from telling Stella to take me home, or I would walk.

Showing my anger, I slammed my backpack on the table and then took my books out and slammed them down.

"Uh oh. What the fuck happened?" Asher asked once he made it to us.

I sighed, and before I could answer, Stella did.

"The hottest guy at the school asked Chloe out. He dumped his girlfriend. Making sure that she wouldn't start things with Chloe before he did it. And she told him she had plans. Plans with me. We can cancel them for Brett. I don't get it."

I sighed, "It's not just that, Stella. I'm not interested in him. He does nothing for me. When I say yes to a guy, I need to feel it in my gut. In my heart, he's the right one for me. I don't want a lot of men. I just want one."

Asher mumbled then, "Nothing wrong with waiting for the right one."

Stella growled, "I know that, Dad. But none of the boys at school pay me a lick of attention. I gotta live vicariously through her. She gets asked out at least three times a week. And she always says no. Either they aren't her type. Too immature. Or she knows at least three other girls the guy has been with."

And I swore I freaking swore I heard Asher mutter, "Good."

But I hadn't... right?

And then my phone pinged with a text.

Unknown – *Hey, so what time should I pick you up?*

Unknown – *I've been wanting to ask you out for a while. But I didn't want Karla's drama to touch you. That's gotta count for something. Right?*

I narrowed my eyes and then looked at Stella, "You freaking didn't."

She looked at me, her eyes wide, "Do what?"

I could feel Asher's eyes on me, but I ignored him, "You didn't give my number to Brett. You wouldn't do that."

Stella winced, "I didn't do that. Exactly."

I could feel my anger mounting, "How, exactly?"

Then she rushed out, "I may have opened my contact book, scrolled to your number, and laid the phone down on the desk in front of him."

I loved Stella. I did.

But she had crossed a line.

Here I was, keeping my feelings to myself.

Doing everything I could think of to not lose her.

I felt a tear trail down the corner of my eye, and then when she caught sight of it, her face paled, Asher muttered, "Fuck."

I stood up, put my stuff back in my backpack, and then looked around Asher and to Stoney I asked, "Can you run me home, please?"

He saw the next tear that trailed down my cheek, then nodded, "Yeah, sweetheart. Let's go."

I ignored Asher and Stella and walked beside Stoney.

When I got home, I headed to my bedroom, closed the door, and then blocked Brett's number.

For the rest of the evening, I worked on my homework. I had to set my phone to the side and was close to turning it off because not only was Stella texting me, but so was Asher.

I ignored the two of them.

After I ate dinner, and thankfully, my mama and dad were busy talking about a cruise that they were thinking of taking in a few years, so I was able to keep everything to myself, I settled into bed and then looked at my phone.

Thirteen missed calls from Stella.

Three from Asher.

Stella – *Co, I'm sorry.*

Stella – *Co, please answer your phone. I shouldn't have done that.*

Stella – *I'm just so frustrated. Because of who my dad is, nobody wants to ask me out.*

Stella – *The amazing friend you are, you would tell me that it means they don't deserve me.*

Stella – *You would be right.*

Asher – *Talk to her, Chloe. She's torn up.*

Stella – *I love you like a fat kid loves cake. I know how you feel, and I am so sorry, Co.*

Stella – *So I don't do it again, I'll delete your number from my phone?*

Stella – *I'll dress up in purple tomorrow.*

Stella hates the color purple.

Stella – *Please forgive me, Co. Please. I won't do this again.*

Asher – *I've talked to her. Let her off the hook for me, yeah?*

I sighed. I knew Stella couldn't help herself, and I knew she was frustrated. But if she did anything like this again, I was egging her car.

And I texted her as much.

Her reply was instantaneous, almost as if she was staring at it.

Stella – *Deal.*

Asher – *Thanks. My ears just bled from her screech.*

Asher – *Do anything to make her smile.*

I smiled at that.

Me – *I know. Me too. But I can't create feelings for someone that aren't there.*

Asher – *And that makes you one admirable person, Chloe. Someone I'm honored to know.*

Then I smiled.

That felt nice.

That caused my body to warm all over.

Then to Stella, I said.

Me – *I forgive you. But you have to wear purple tomorrow.*

It was the very next day, and since today was Friday, and since we were old enough now, and our parents were okay with it, we were leaving at noon since it was a half day, swinging by the clubhouse, then heading to Badd Motha Ink and getting our noses pierced.

We both had been begging to have it done.

And since Badd Motha Ink did all the ink for Zagan MC, they were happy to do it.

The moment I walked out of my house and headed to Stella's car, she jumped out and showed me her outfit.

I stared for a beat, then two, then three, then laughed so hard I almost peed on myself.

She had on a purple bandana around her head, a purple long-sleeved shirt, purple athletic shorts, purple knee-high socks, and purple tennis shoes.

"I love you, and I'm sorry." She said as she reached me.

I grinned, "I know, I love you too. You brought a change of clothes, right?"

She nodded.

I smiled, then took a picture and gestured to the house, "Go change."

She spun so fast her ponytail hit my face, and then she opened the car door, grabbed her bag, and raced into the house.

I snickered and then pulled up Asher's number.

I brought the phone to my ear, and he answered on the second ring, "You okay?"

I grinned, "How long did y'all have to shop for that purple stuff?"

He laughed, "Show you the video of it later. Funniest shit I've ever seen."

I giggled.

We hung up, and then Stella came racing out of my house in her normal clothes of ripped jeans, a band tee, and her Converse, the same as me.

The moment we pulled into the parking lot, I looked up and felt my jaw drop, then I looked at Stella and asked, "What is Pagan doing here?"

She snickered, "Dad's orders. Come on. You'll see."

I nodded, then climbed out of the car.

Pagan jerked his chin up at us and then walked behind us to the front steps.

Then, I caught sight of Brett and his friends.

The moment he saw us, he smiled and then headed in our direction.

But he didn't make it close.

Because one second, Pagan was behind us, and then he was right in front of us, "That's far enough. Chloe told you she wasn't interested. You need to respect that. You don't, we're going to have problems."

Brett showed that he had been tackled one too many times when he bowed up at Pagan, "Yeah, and who the fuck are you. This is between me and Chloe."

Pagan shook his head, "I'm the fucker that was sent here to talk to you. You need to play the hand that's been dealt. Because if you keep on playing, you're going to be dealt a losing hand. And you won't like it. I guarantee you that."

Stella snickered, then looked at me, "I know this is my fault. I really am sorry."

I shrugged, "It's okay. I get it."

Brett opened his mouth and said, "Look, I get it. Okay. I do. But I've had my eye on Chloe for years. I was just too stupid to realize it. I just want a chance."

Pagan looked over his shoulder at me and lifted a brow.

I shook my head, then looked at Brett, "I'm really not interested. You're not going to change my mind, so please, don't try."

Pagan looked at Brett, "There you have it. Leave her the fuck alone."

One of Brett's friends, Kent, asked, "You her boyfriend or something?"

Pagan snorted. "No. I'm not stupid. No way in fuck am I getting my ass killed for thinking about Chloe in any way other than family."

And with that, he looked at Brett, "This is your only warning. You don't want to have to deal with the Pres."

Brett sighed, then nodded.

Huh, guess he did have a few brain cells left.

Then I looked at Stella, "What did he mean? Deal with the Pres?"

She shrugged, "No clue."

With that, Pagan looked at us, jerked his chin, then headed to his bike.

All through the day, everyone was whispering about the girl who turned Brett down. I got more looks than I ever have before.

And I also got more looks for the guys at school than I ever had before. Most of those consisted of top-to-toe looks. Lingering on my boobs and my butt. Ugh, I rolled my eyes at the last guy. Gross.

When were they going to learn that there was more to a woman than the way her body looked... probably not until they were fifty or so.

But... what had us laughing our asses off... while we were headed to her car, we passed Brett with his arm thrown over Karla's shoulders.

I looked at Stella, she looked at me, and then we started laughing.

Once we made it to the clubhouse to ask Asher to make the call, I went to the fridge, grabbed two grape sodas, and then made sandwiches.

Stella came in as I was putting the cheese on them, and then she settled on the bar stool and popped the tabs, "Dad's in church. As soon as he gets out, I'll ask him to make the call."

I nodded.

My mom and dad were okay with it, and I even had a written form of consent with their numbers on it.

We ate and talked about the kind of jewelry we wanted. Stella wanted a diamond stud, and I wanted the black nose ring.

We had just finished our last bites when Asher walked into the kitchen in faded jeans, motorcycle boots, and a dark blue tee underneath his kutte.

His face was hard, and I could tell that he had run his hand through his hair.

His eyes went to Stella, then they came to me, and not realizing I was doing it, I tilted my head and asked, "Are you okay?"

He sighed, which caused Stella to really look at him.

He nodded, "Yeah. Be alright."

Then he looked at Stella, "What did you need, princess?"

Stella smiled wide, then, "We wanted you to call over to Badd Motha Ink and see if they can fit us in."

He lifted a brow, "For what?"

Stella smiled, "We want to get our noses pierced."

He looked at me, and I nodded.

He sighed, then ran his hand through his hair again, and that clued me in that he was way stressed out, but just like the man he was, he asked, "Who do you plan to do it?"

Stella laughed, "Really, Daddy? Do you honestly think we would go to anyone other than Alise?"

He nodded, "Good."

Once he placed the call, Stella hugged him and pressed a kiss to his cheek.

I didn't do that.

No, I headed to the pantry and moved a few boxes around until I found the stash I had hidden.

Then I tagged a *Reese Cup* and hid the stash again.

Then I walked it over to Asher. "These always seem to make you feel better."

He looked at me, then down at my hand, and then I watched as the corners of his eyes crinkled. He whispered one word, "Thanks."

After we got our noses pierced, we picked up a pizza, went back to the clubhouse, and settled into the media room Asher had added to the clubhouse last year.

I smiled at Stella when she popped in the first DVD of my favorite series.

She was still trying to get back into my good graces, and with this, she was definitely there.

But I snickered when she started snoring ten minutes into the second episode.

Just then, two of the club girls who had joined the club walked by the media room.

And I wanted to weep for Adeline and her story.

It was heartbreaking. Everything that poor woman had gone through.

But I knew that I didn't know everything. And honestly, I don't think I ever did.

However, I will say this. Even though I was sure she had gone through some of the worst things a female can go through, they all made her into the amazing woman she is today.

And just like Adeline, there was Sutton.

She was another one of the club girls who had joined and had captured the attention of one man, and when he finally pulled his head out of his behind, I knew it was going to be explosive.

And I was all here for it.

Well... as much as I could be, at least.

Chapter 4

Asher – Past – Age 38

I was still staring at that *Reese Cup* Chloe had handed to me hours later.

I probably did need to eat it.

But something stopped me from doing that.

She was all the time doing little things like that.

And without rhyme or reason, I grabbed a sharpie, wrote the date on it, opened the drawer I had the others in, and carefully placed it there.

Seeing the ones she had given me over the years, I smiled, then closed the drawer.

There was a knock on my office door.

I called out, "Yeah?"

Charlie opened the door and then headed inside.

"I'm not sure who she has helping her, but no fucking luck, Pres. You want me to get with Hippie, just say the word."

I leaned back in my chair and sighed, "Just keep looking for her. I trust you, Charlie. I know you'll find her."

He nodded, then walked out of my office.

Closing my eyes, I tried to think of anywhere that she could be.

This shit was getting old real fucking fast.

It's been sixteen years since I laid eyes on her.

Knowing her, I was surprised now that I think about how long it's been.

And add into that how long it's been since we've dealt with *Verity Runner's MC,* which I thought we had dismantled years ago when I started this MC.

VRMC was a one percent motorcycle club like we were.

However, where we drew the line at hurting kids and women, they didn't have such lines.

Therefore, we dismantled them before Stella was born because no way in fucking hell was I going to allow an MC that was all about trafficking kids to be in the same world that my daughter lived in, we were able to save seventy-nine children.

But we had gotten word from one of our informants that we didn't get all the members like we thought we had.

The president... a man everyone referred to as El Toro, no one knew his real name, had apparently gone to ground.

But he was back in the land of the living.

Needing to get my mind off where my thoughts were headed, I got out of my office and walked through the clubhouse.

As soon as I saw the glow from the media room I had installed a year ago, I headed in that direction.

A year ago, Stella and Chloe wanted to go see a double feature at the theater.

And I had been all for it, and it had been fine for years.

Until I saw two of the attendees eyeing the girls up and down when they were only thirteen years old.

I had threatened the two punks to within an inch of their life.

But that hadn't stopped them when the girls went the following weekend again.

That was why I had the media room built.

And boy, but it got fucking used.

That made it easier not to sweat over the ten grand I had shelled out.

But what really made it worth it? Seeing the smiles on the girl's faces at Christmas time in their pajamas and fuzzy blankets.

I walked to the media room and saw Chloe's eyes light on the television, and Stella was fast asleep.

I didn't question it as my feet carried my body to the recliner beside the couch, where they were settled.

But first, I grabbed two throws, covered Stella up, and then handed one to Chloe.

She smiled, "Thank you."

I settled into the recliner, then kicked back.

"What are we watching?" I asked Chloe.

She smiled, "The Last Ship."

I nodded.

I've never sat down and watched it. But I've heard Chloe talking about it.

And when I felt eyes on me, I looked at Chloe.

"You're really going to watch it?" She asked.

I nodded, "Yep."

She smiled, "Well, okay then."

And I wanted to kick my ass for not watching this show sooner. It was pretty damn good.

My eyes stayed glued to the episode called Gitmo.

Then I mumbled, "I want to be like Tex when I grow up."

And when I didn't hear anything, I looked over at Chloe, and sure enough, she was out like a light.

Her mouth was partially open, and a little drool was pooling on the couch cushion.

I held in my chuckle.

Carefully, I got up and covered her up, then moved to Stella, pulled her blanket up higher, and pressed a kiss to the crown of her head.

After I killed the lights in the media room, I headed to the main room and looked at Whit, "Keep it down tonight. Girls are asleep in the media room."

He lifted his chin.

There was an unspoken rule in this club.

It didn't matter if we had important people here.

It didn't matter if it was a big night.

If kids were asleep, shit got toned down.

And I loved the hell out of it.

It was three weeks later when it happened again.

Sometimes, she would come to me, sit down, and ask a random question.

Sometimes, I would go over to where she was and ask her if she had any random thoughts.

But it never bothered me who was around when she did this.

Because I didn't let it matter.

We were having a party as well as a meeting to discuss a new trafficking ring that had popped up, and I knew deep in my bones that it was the Verity Runner's MC.

Because this trafficking ring wasn't centralized in just one area.

Oh no, it was cluing a lot of people in that they were operating in the south.

Which was uncommon as all hell.

Because people in the South were known for being gun owners and not being afraid to use them.

We were all outside, eight of us in total, with a few members from each motorcycle club making sure that no one got close enough to hear what we were discussing.

Yes, we could have met up in church, but the room wasn't near large enough to house everyone and them not be on top of one another.

Powers, the president of the Tennessee chapter of Wrath MC, was in attendance.

Cotton, the national president, was supposed to be here, but his daughter, who played Volleyball, was in the championship playoffs.

Declan, the president of the Alabama chapter of Wrath MC.

Storm, the president of the South Carolina chapter of Wrath MC.

Trident, the president of the Georgia chapter of Wrath MC.

Teague is a member of the Texas chapter of Wrath MC.

Raptor is a member of the Florida chapter of Wrath MC.

Vulcan is the vice president of Immoral Saints MC out of Georgia.

Nuke, the president of the Soulless Outlaws MC out of Louisiana.

Tomb, the president of the Pagan's Soldiers MC out of Kentucky.

"I'm telling you, we need to get ahead of this shit before it explodes in our faces," Powers said as he took a pull from his beer.

I nodded, "Yeah. They nabbed a teenage girl a few towns over. Parents are beside themselves."

"Anyone have any leads?" Powers asked.

Declan shook his head, "No fucking clue. But me and the boys have our ears to the ground."

I lifted my chin, "I got a feeling about who it could be, but I need proof before I bring this shit to the proverbial table."

Tomb nodded his head, "Yeah, a few kids have gone missing in our area too. Two girls and one boy. Ages range from eight to twelve."

Vulcan said, "Yeah, that's about the same age range we're seeing too."

Nuke sighed, "What I want to know is how are they getting this fucking information?"

Teague jerked up his chin, "We're researching that. But we think they have someone from social services in each state that's giving them this information."

Trident nodded, "We're thinking the same thing. Cause the four kids that were grabbed from our area are kids that no one would miss. Two of them were in the system, and the other two are living with parents who don't give a shit."

I nodded, "I'll have Charlie check to see if that's the case with the ones we found out were taken."

I felt her before I saw her.

The way my spine tingled, the way proverbial butterflies took flight in my belly.

I tilted my head to the side and locked eyes with hers.

She had that look on her face when something was bothering her.

Her eyebrows were scrunched together, and she was nibbling on her lower lip.

Seeing that, I did the only thing I could do; I called out, "Chloe, come on over here and tell me what's on your mind."

When she got closer, she shook her head, "No, you're busy. It can wait."

I shook my head, "It doesn't matter. What is it?"

She sighed, then took in the men who were sitting in chairs and the men who were standing around.

Once her eyes came back to mine, she walked over, then knelt to the side of my chair and said, "You know how some gravesites hold someone's plot for a certain number of years after they die?"

I nodded, "Yeah. What about it?"

She asked, "What do you think they do with the coffins and the bodies?"

I thought about it for a moment and then shook my head, "I got no fucking clue."

Tomb spoke up then, "They recycle the coffins. As for the bodies, there's nothing left."

Chloe shivered, "Yeah, I wanna be cremated and my headstone to be placed overlooking a cliff."

I chuckled, "Yeah, sounds a lot better.'"

She nodded, "Yeah, it definitely does."

Then she got up, and like the fool I was where she was concerned, I watched her go.

Trying to bite back the growl of her in those short fucking shorts.

She was lucky it was so hot outside today that I couldn't tell her to go change.

"She single?" Vulcan asked.

I skewered him with a look that said I would carve his eyes from his skull if she dared to look at her again, then growled, "She's only seven-fucking-teen."

He nodded, "You tell yourself that every second of the day?"

I didn't say anything to that.

Instead, I said, "I'm hoping to have more concrete proof of who I think is behind it." Then I looked at Teague, "Charlie couldn't figure out the name of a certain man. No matter the channels he used, neither could Hippie. I think Miller might be able to figure it out."

Teague jerked up his chin.

After we went a few more rounds, so to speak, everyone stood and agreed to share any information.

My eyes scanned the area, and when I found Stella near the tables, I looked for Chloe, who was on the other end placing down platters of food she had probably cooked.

I knew what area I was going to be demolishing here in a bit.

But first, I needed a fucking beer.

Conleigh

The man I had been introduced to as Asher, I don't think he realized that the look he had sent to a young girl had gone unnoticed. Seeing his jaw ticking and the fist around his beer bottle tightening when some other man had sat down beside the young girl?

That was the look of a possessed alpha man if I have ever seen one. Sure, I've seen that look from the brothers of Wrath MC and even from Gage, but none of them has been quite like this look.

She was gorgeous in a girl-next-door kind of way. And the girl sitting beside her. Now that I'm getting a closer look at her, she resembles Asher. Perhaps that's his daughter? Maybe?

Then, who was the girl that Asher was looking at?

Then it hit me. That must be his daughter's best friend… oh shit.

But that wasn't the oh shit moment, well, it was, but not entirely.

The man who had sat down beside the girl reached over and moved a stray of her hair that had come loose from her bun back behind her ear.

Well, that's what it looked like he was in the process of… until she pulled her head away from him.

The man at our sides stood and then slammed his beer on the table to storm over there.

"Where is the popcorn when you need it?" I asked the girls who had joined me about half an hour ago.

Lil looked up from her chips and salsa and asked, "What?"

June nodded, "You are so right."

"Hot baby Jesus." Harlow breathed out.

Michelle and Mackenzie both said at the same time, "We need Twizzlers for this, too."

"Get. The. Fuck. Up." Each word that came out of Asher's mouth was with a growl.

We all sat there watching this unfold, and the stupid idiot crossed his arms over his chest and literally said, "Last time I checked, you ain't a member of this club. Means you can't tell me to fucking move."

"Last time I checked, boy? The last motherfucker that spoke to me like that had the opportunity to find out why I used to be known as Breaker. Furthermore, this is my motherfucking club. This is my god damned house. I tell you to the fuck up, you fucking do it."

Apparently, none of the women at our table knew that answer. Oh, but the men sure did.

In fact, a few of them went over there and moved the younger man away from the girls. "This is bullshit. I saw her first." The boy was yelling at him.

We couldn't hear what was said, but apparently, Asher got his point across when the young man's eyes widened, and his face paled.

The moment Asher stepped back, the younger man bolted out of the clubhouse like his ass was on fire.

I watched as the younger girl stepped away from them, walked to a cooler, grabbed a beer, then walked back to the man and handed it to him.

But you can bet there was no mistaking the heat in the man's eyes as he gazed at the younger woman.

Was everyone else here blind to it?

Or did they all know that he was waiting until she was legal?

Would it be possible to become a fly on the wall for this?

Chapter 5

Chloe – Past – Age 18

"You look beautiful, Mija," my mama said as she finished curling the last strand of my hair.

This year has flown by, and since it was New Year's, I was about to head to the clubhouse for the annual New Year's Eve party.

Every year, my mama curled my hair for the event. Since it was so long, it made more sense.

I smiled, "Thank you, Mama. And thank you for my good genes."

She winked at me, "So, are you planning on getting a New Year kiss from anyone?"

I gasped, "Mama? Really?"

She chuckled, "I kissed your father. That was how I knew he was the one."

I thought about what she said for a few minutes.

And when I looked in the mirror at her, I could tell that she knew something.

She was my mama, after all.

And she proved that when she said, "I know, Mija. I know. But Stella loves you. She will forgive you. I think the greatest harm anyone can do to themselves is to deny what the heart wants. No one wants to be miserable."

"There's a big age difference," I said.

She shrugged, "The heart wants what it wants. As long as God is pleased with you, then the opinions of others don't matter."

Her words stayed with me while I got ready.

But they almost left my head when I walked down the steps and saw that my dad's friend, Marco, was seated on the couch, and they were watching a game.

I wasn't sure what it was about him, but he gave me the major creeps.

Perhaps it was the predatory way his eyes moved up and down my body.

The predatory look in that he wouldn't mind taking what wasn't offered to him freely.

Thankfully, my mama caught my eye and gestured for me to go ahead and leave.

Her words stayed with me until I climbed in my car, a little Honda Civic that was my eighteenth birthday present from my parents.

The moment I pulled into the club's parking lot, I drove around groups of bikes until I pulled my car in beside Stella's.

I thought it was awesome when Asher showed me that I had a designated parking spot.

Speaking of Asher.

My fingers trailed over the little pendant that was attached to a white gold chain around my neck.

He had gifted me the necklace on my birthday.

And that little pendant... well, if you didn't know what it was, then you wouldn't know what it was.

It was in the shape of fireworks.

Something I didn't know the meaning behind.

And neither did Stella.

Asher wouldn't tell me about the meaning behind it, no matter how many times I had begged to be told.

I sighed then and climbed out of my car, only to feel guilty as all got out when I caught sight of Stella, who was smiling at me while walking over to me.

I forced a smile, and when she tilted her head, I knew she saw it.

Dang it.

Just as she opened her mouth to say something, Gabby came over and smiled, "Thank goodness. We need help in the kitchen."

And just like that, we headed into the clubhouse, but not before Stella leaned in and said, "I want to know what's going on."

I sighed, then nodded, and while I cooked, I tried to think about a lie that she would believe.

And I hated it.

I hated lying for one thing.

I hated lying worst of all to Stella.

But I couldn't tell her this. I just freaking couldn't.

We had just finished getting everything done and ready, and just in time, too.

Because the masses were hungry.

I had just carried one dish to the bar top.

Since it was cold outside, we wouldn't be eating outside like we did nine times out of ten.

Once I set the dish on the bar top, I tilted my head, and at that feeling, I winced, then raced to the bathroom.

Why, oh, why didn't I check my app before I left the house?

I bought a brand-new box yesterday, knowing it was getting close to time for my period.

Pulling my phone out of my back pocket, I opened my messages to Stella.

Me – *Do you have any tampons?*

I sat there and waited.

And waited.

And freaking waited.

And when she didn't respond, I texted Gabby.

Gabby was short for Gabriella.

She was one of the new club girls the club had hired, and I adored her.

She was older than me by at least three years, but she was awesome.

Me – *Hey, do you have any tampons?*

Thankfully, she responded quickly.

Gabby – *No. Sorry. I used my last one a few days ago. Stella?*

Me – *She hasn't texted me back yet.*

I sat there and waited.

My phone buzzed then.

Gabby – *Stella's phone died. But she doesn't have any.*

I shook my head; this was going to be torture.

But I pulled my big girl panties up, so to speak, and grabbed a lot of toilet paper for a makeshift pad.

Just as I was about to place it in my underwear, my phone buzzed again.

And when I saw the message, my face flamed.

Asher – *What do you need?*

No way in all get out was I telling him.

I would die of mortification.

Me – *Nothing. It's fine.*

I put my phone down on the floor and then placed the toilet paper.

Wiped, stood, carefully pulled up my underwear, making sure the toilet paper didn't move, then pulled up my jeans and flushed.

I had just finished washing my hands when my phone buzzed.

Asher – *Talked to Gabby and Stella. Sit tight. Be back.*

Umm.... what?

I called him.

It rang. And rang. And.... "Yeah?"

I sighed, "What do you mean sit tight and you will be back?"

"You need something. Headed to get it." He said without an ounce of sarcasm.

My heart melted while my face flamed yet again, how in the world was that possible?

Those two things happening at the same time?

I ran a hand through my hair and said, "Asher, you don't have to do that."

I heard his blinker come on, "Be back in less than ten minutes. You wanna stay on the phone with me until I get the ones you need?"

I leaned against the wall in the bathroom and nodded, even though he couldn't see me, "Yeah. Thank you, Asher."

"Ain't a thing." I heard his truck shut off, and then his door opened and closed.

I was fiddling with the hem on my blouse when he said, "So, what else do you need?"

My fingers froze, and then I lifted a brow, "Besides tampons?"

He answered, "Yeah."

I thought for a minute, then said, "Umm, well, Midol and candy. Anything that's chocolate."

"Got it. Okay, hang on, Chloe," he said, then spoke to someone, "Yeah, can you tell me where the tampons are and where the Midol is?"

I didn't hear anything after that, but I did hear Asher mutter, "Thanks." ... then I heard, "Not on your fucking life."

"What?" I asked.

"The woman thought it was hot that a man would buy tampons for someone. Said that was the kind of man she'd like to get to know. Blondes don't do a thing for me."

Whether it was the cramp that just assaulted my body or something else, I didn't know, but I opened my mouth and asked, "What does it for you?"

He answered immediately, "Dark-haired, green-eyed beauties. Okay, I'm at the tampons. What kind do you want?"

My breath lodged in my throat. Deep in my throat at his words.

Because those were me.

Oh. My. Gawd.

I didn't realize I hadn't replied to him until I heard, "Chloe?"

I shook my head, then blurted out, "Sorry. Umm, I usually get the blue box and regular."

"Got it. Okay. Be back in less than six minutes." And with that, he hung up the phone.

I let my hand drop, still clutching my phone, and again heard the words in his raspy tone: *Dark-haired, green-eyed beauties.*

Then I heard my mama's words again: *The heart wants what it wants. As long as God is pleased with you, the opinions of others don't matter.*

I didn't know how long I stood there until there was a knock on the door.

I walked over to it, unlocked it, opened it, and took the box Asher was holding. "Got your other stuff for you. Come find me when you get done."

And with that, he turned on his boot and walked away.

I wanted to watch him walk away, but alas, the toilet paper wasn't cutting it.

After I did what I needed to do, I walked out of the bathroom, the box of tampons underneath my arm, and with my head held high, I walked into the main room of the clubhouse.

Stella met me, then took the box from me, and said, "That little cabinet in the bathroom, Dad said for me to put them in there and add tampons to the weekly shopping list... Go eat. Dad made your plate for you."

I nodded, then said, "Thank you."

My eyes landed on Asher right away, and I headed in his direction, he saw me coming and then jerked his head to a plate of food that was sitting beside his.

I sat down then whispered, "Thank you."

He winked at me and then nodded.

After we all ate, we headed outside to watch the fireworks the MC put on every year.

I was curled up in a lawn chair underneath a blanket beside Asher, with Stella on the other side of him.

"Do you think it's possible to push out a uterus through your vagina?" I asked Asher as another cramp assaulted my body.

Asher being Asher, he didn't laugh. He didn't snicker.

No, he leaned down and picked up the bag I hadn't noticed he had.

He opened it up and pulled out a bottle of grape soda, opened it, handed it to me, and then he opened the box of Midol, read the instructions, shook two out, and handed them to me.

Once I took them and drank some of the soda, he then reached into the bag and pulled out a smaller bag of my favorite candy.

The *Snickers* with almonds in them.

He unwrapped one and handed it to me.

Stella chimed in, "Oh, gimmie one."

He looked at her after he handed me the *Snickers* and asked, "Are you on your period?"

She shook her head.

"Then you don't get one." Then he pulled out a smaller bag of her favorite candy, *Three Musketeers,* and handed it to her.

After I popped the chocolate in my mouth, I ate it and then felt my breath catch again when Asher leaned over and whispered, "If I could go through it for you, I fucking would."

I could say that so many things that this man had done that had caused me to fall in love with him.

But at his words and the sincerity in them... I fell even harder.

And I would be damned if I chased after my feelings and ruined my relationship with Stella.

But apparently, Asher hadn't said what he did low enough.

Because someone had heard it, and they smiled.

Because it was about time.

If they had to watch the whole star-crossed lover's thing, and nothing became of it, they were going to revolt.

Perhaps it was time to move those two along.

I didn't get my New Year's Eve kiss like I had been thinking about.

There was only one person I wanted it from.

And I didn't have the courage nor the want to blow my friendship with Stella wide open and ruin anything.

***

But all of that almost became one of the biggest lies I'd ever told.

It was the week before prom. And Stella and I had agreed to be each other's date.

We were at her house getting ready.

P!nk was in the background singing about *Beautiful Trauma* while I did my make-up.

We both went yesterday and had our nails done.

Thankfully, I had just finished with my last swipe of mascara when Stella shouted, "That's bullcrap."

I turned my head to look at her, "What happened?"

"There was water damage at the event, so we are having it at the school gym."

I frowned. "Shouldn't they have known about this five hours before the event?"

She nodded, "I know, right? That's sketch."

And it was sketch.

She sat down and then said, "I don't want our prom to be at the gym."

Then I got an idea in my head and asked, "Do you remember years ago for your tenth birthday, and you wanted a fairy party? Do you think they still have the lights and stuff?"

Her eyes got wide, then she hit a button and put the phone on speaker.

I heard Asher's voice shortly after that, "Everything okay, princess?"

"They changed the event to the gym. And that doesn't sound like fun. Chloe thought about my tenth birthday. Do y'all still have the lights and stuff?"

He was quiet for a beat, then said, "When will the two of you be ready?"

Stella answered him, "Forty-five minutes or so."

I nodded.

"Okay. Tell you what, y'all finish getting ready, I'm going to have Gabby grab y'all dinner. Eat that. Then I'll send someone to pick y'all up. Don't worry about a thing. Alright?"

She nodded.

Then, before she hung up, I heard Asher ask, "Color's your dress, princess?"

"Light blue."

Then he asked, "Chloe's?"

"Deep red."

He was silent for another beat, then said, "Okay." And with that, he hung up.

After we got ready, Gabby knocked on the door. Stella answered it, and I heard, "Dayum girl, you are looking fine."

Stella beamed.

Then I saw Gabby, and when she saw me, her jaw dropped, then closed, then dropped again, then she said, "Girl... holy shit. Are you planning to give the brothers a heart attack?"

Stella snickered, "I made her get it. She looks stunning in it."

"It's too much," I said.

The same thing I said to Stella when she made me try it on at the store a couple of months ago.

"It is not. Now let's see what Dad got us." We both thanked Gabby and then she was out the door.

And it was our favorite.

Italian dishes from *Italiano's*, the best Italian restaurant in the state. If you wanted my opinion and basically that of everyone in our county.

My mouth watered when I smelled everything.

And then, my senses were heightened when I took my first bite of the creamy Tuscan chicken pasta.

Stella got the chicken carbonara, her favorite as well.

And the garlic bread delish.

I was so full I didn't think I could move.

Well, that was until we both heard the sounds of Harley pipes.

I looked at Stella.

She looked at me.

And we grinned, "Way out," I whispered.

"Righteous," she whispered back.

Once we made it to the door, we both stood and waited.

We didn't have to wait long.

Because there was a knock on the door.

Stella opened the door, and my breath caught at Asher.

He had smoothed his hair back.

A black button-up, dark jeans, and his kutte.

And the man that was standing at his side, wait... was that?

I looked at Stella to see her cheeks were pink.

Umm, how in the world was Asher okay with this?

But I got my answer.

"Since it's prom, figure it's okay. Stella, you can ride Kyrian."

Stella tried but failed and smiled big.

She's had a crush on the man since the first time she saw him.

That was the real reason why she tried to hook me up with guys in high school.

She hoped that one of them would be good enough and would have a friend, and she would be able to work out her infatuation with Kyrian. Seeing as he was twelve years older than she was.

But she had nothing to fear compared to the age difference between me and my crush.

But my eyes were back on Kyrian, who jerked his chin at Stella.

Kyrian. A man with no last name.

A silent man who did amazing ink.

A man who did amazing ink at almost six foot four.

A six-foot-four bald-headed man.

And now I knew why he was here.

Because Kyrian was the only tattoo artist, Creature would let work on him. And Creature being Creature, who wasn't a fan of enclosed spaces.

My eyes moved to Kyrian's shirt, and when I saw a light blue flower pinned to his shirt, I smiled, and when I looked at Asher's kutte and saw the same thing but a deep red flower, I smiled even harder.

Asher asked, "Are you ladies ready to go to prom?"

We both nodded.

Kyrian stood to the side, as did Asher.

Once we passed them, Stella started down the stairs, and I followed.

We made it to their bikes, and Asher leaned in and said, "The way you look in that dress, no way in hell should it be wasted. So, climb on."

So that was what I did, but not before he said, "Mind your heels and the pipes, Chloe."

I nodded.

The moment I was settled behind him, he said over the rumble of his bike, "Going to keep it slow so your hair doesn't get ruined, alright?"

I wrapped my arms around his middle and said, "Sounds good."

I looked over at Stella, who had her eyes on me, and she mouthed, "Oh my gawd."

I giggled, and thankfully, it was drowned out by Asher's bike.

When we pulled out of the driveway, we were met with ten members of Zagan MC, along with Hugo, Archer, and Hale, the other three artists that make up Badd Motha Ink.

As we passed the entrance to the school, I was kind of shocked. The parking lot was half full.

But what I thought was funny was that we passed a restaurant, and I saw Brett walking in front of Karla.

Did anyone tell her she looked like the big bird on that show Sesame Street?

Geez, she needed some new friends.

Once we made it to the clubhouse, Asher backed his bike in and then shut it off.

Placing my hand on his shoulder, I carefully stood, then watched as he moved and looked me up and down, "Yeah, hair is still good."

I smiled up at him, "Thank you, Asher."

He nodded, "Just don't revert to that Mr. Hendrix shit. Alright?"

I giggled, then nodded.

Stella was walking at Kyrian's side; however, she stepped closer to me, wrapped her arm in mine, and whispered, "Can we freeze time, please? I wanted to remain on the back of his bike for the rest of eternity."

I snickered, not saying that I wanted to do that too with Asher.

We walked into the clubhouse, and we both stopped and stared.

The entire clubhouse was transformed with fairy lights.

The tables and chairs had been moved.

The dance floor was created.

Little paper lanterns hung from the ceiling.

Little plates and cups littered the bar top with what appeared to be finger foods.

Asher and Kyrian stepped around us and headed farther into the main room of the clubhouse.

Just then, I heard a squeal.

I was shocked when I saw Casey, Nora, Poppy, Lizzie, and Maria. I looked at Stella, who was smiling.

"Texted them while you were doing your finishing touches. They thought the gym was a bad idea, too."

I nodded.

Just then, Whit came over the speaker and said, "Will the following ladies please report to the men who have a flower that matches the color of your dress?"

I smiled.

Together, the seven of us headed to the dance floor.

Stella went to Kyrian.

Nora went to Trigger.

Casey went to Pagan.

Lizzie went to Irish.

Maria went to Priest.

And I went to Asher.

He wrapped his arm around my waist, I placed my hand in his, and then the music started.

The seven of us busted up laughing when the song *Good Girls Go Bad* came on.

Asher leaned down and whispered, "I'm glad y'all didn't go."

I lifted a brow and whispered back, "And why is that?"

He shrugged, "Because if anyone made you uncomfortable, they'd be six feet under."

I felt a chill sweep over my spine.

And I had to fight the urge to lean up on my tiptoes and press my lips to his.

God, but I wanted nothing more.

Stella. Stella. Stella.

This was insane.

I know the words my mother said to me.

But how much longer would it be until I reached my breaking point where this man was concerned?

After we danced and danced and danced, and drank so much punch and danced some more, we were all fielding calls and texts asking where we were.

We weren't telling a soul.

We danced for so long that I had to take my heels off and go barefoot.

But what had me close to crying was the last dance of the night when a song I'd never heard before started playing, and Asher tugged me onto the dance floor.

And when he sang these lyrics, *I will wait for you, Til' the sun burns into ashes and bows down to the moon I will wait for you...* I knew... I knew I had just reached my breaking point.

I searched those lyrics, found the song, and listened to it while I cried myself to sleep.

***

And for the next year, even though I tried to distance myself from the club and Asher, I didn't miss anything that took place.

A nomad had returned to the club a man named Pipe.

And instant sparks flew between Pipe and Gabby.

I was so happy for her.

And even more so when they got married and they were currently waiting to welcome their son into the world.

Also, Coal finally claimed Adeline.

And yes, Irish finally pulled his head out of his behind where Sutton was concerned. He had to do a lot of groveling, but I was so glad that she was back.

And the daughter that Irish never knew about and was abandoned at the gates of the club was cute as a button. The bond that Sutton had with Maisie was something out of a fairytale.

I couldn't be happier for them all.

But I wanted what they all had. What they had all found, which was why, over the next couple of months, I had tried to distance myself even more from wanting and needing to see Asher every day.

But I had done it.

Thankfully, since we had graduated, and Stella was in cosmetology school, and I was in school for accounting since I loved numbers, we didn't go to the clubhouse all that often.

So, I didn't see him all that often.

But I did allow myself to text Asher with random thoughts.

Like last week.

Me – *How is a banana a berry, but a strawberry isn't?*

Asher – *Excuse me?*

Me – *Yeah. According to Google.*

Asher – *Berry is in its name.*

One week later...

Me – *Did you know that octopuses have three hearts?*

Asher – *Fuck. That would make for a hard surgery.*

Three weeks after that.

Asher – *Why aren't you coming to the clubhouse?*

Me – *School is kicking my behind.*

Asher – *You want to lie to yourself, alright? But don't lie to me.*

Me – *Okay. The reason behind it is mine alone.*

Me – *Want to tell me why you were covered in blood a few days ago?*

Asher – *Can't.*

Me – *Right.*

I missed him.

God did I miss him.

Stella looked up from the new products she missed at my sigh, one I didn't realize I had let out, and asked, "Everything okay?"

I nodded, "Yeah. Just thinking."

She nodded, but I caught her looking at me with a questioning brow.

I sighed, "Okay, I like someone. But it can never happen."

And she replied with a simple phrase my mama has told me before, too many times to count... "Never say never."

Chapter 6

Asher – Past – Age 39

You know, way back when Barbie first came out.

It was the epitome of the perfect woman.

Blonde hair. Blue eyes. Hourglass figure?

See, when Stella was younger, she loved Barbie dolls.

Loved creating tales with them.

And more times than I could count, I found myself playing with her in her bedroom.

A man isn't a man at all if he isn't willing to do that with his daughter.

And a man isn't a man at all if he isn't willing to play Barbie dolls with his daughter's best friend in the whole wide world.

Chloe was that to Stella.

Through and fucking through.

I couldn't have ordered a better friend for my girl.

And now that she was nineteen... I didn't feel like such a piece of shit for the very few random thoughts I had about her over the years.

I meant what I said in those lyrics I sang to her during the prom night we threw for the girls.

I will wait for her.

I was at war.

Working my ass off by being there for her whenever she needed.

Wanting her to see that everything she could ever want, I had it.

Strong shoulders to carry her burdens.

Strong arms when she couldn't walk anymore.

A strong heart that loves his club and his daughter, but a heart that has areas that have been locked since I took my first breath.

Those areas... Chloe carved her name into them without even trying.

And as I sit here, my eyes closed, the memory of Chloe on her prom night in that deep red dress, hugging her body just right, showing off her curves.

That deep v that showed hints of her cleavage.

The length of material that hid her body... her nickname blew into my mind like the most forceful of winds.

Doll Baby.

Well, Doll Baby, you better stay that mindset that you're a one-man kind of woman because I'll be claiming you.

You've always been mine.

And you're going to be mine until the stars fall from the sky and that spark that burns so bright inside you loses its shine.

When Chloe pulled away from the club, it felt like a physical ache... but I didn't regret letting my feelings known to her.

She needed to know them.

To one, come to terms with us.

To two, get ready.

And to three, to know that I was willing to wait for her.

Because a day where I didn't see Chloe, it felt as though my entire world hadn't started.

Chapter 7

Chloe – Past – Age 21

I've been doing good over the last two years.

I loved my new job, and I knew, barring anything happening to the office or my boss, that I planned to work there for a really long time.

I was six months away from being able to get an apartment.

Stella and I had talked about getting a place together... but something had held me back.

Mainly, there was no way I could hide my feelings from her about Asher.

It would be dang near impossible.

And... there was something going on with Stella.

And I didn't know how to bring it up with her.

Especially since I have been keeping a massive secret from her.

But... well... ever since prom, she hasn't talked about Kyrian.

At freaking all.

And three months ago, I found out why.

Kyrian had gotten married to a girl from his past. A girl who he said was his one that got away.

But between you and me, he would have been better off without that woman in his life.

I knew that was mean of me to say, but there was something about her that I couldn't put my finger on. I just didn't like her.

As for Stella, well, apparently, she had a massive crush on someone else.

A brother from another club. His name was Gavel. And he was a brother in the Soulless Outlaws MC.

He was only ten years older than her.

Which was nothing compared to the twenty-one-year difference between Asher and me.

And just thinking about him... it was making it hard. So, so hard.

Even more reason for me to distance myself.

It's been hard, but I've been doing it.

There have been times when I wanted to talk to Stella and see what she thinks.

There have been times that I wanted to talk to Asher and see if the massive uncontrollable feelings I have for that man are only one-sided.

But like every birthday we've had since we met, we've either celebrated it at Stella's house or here at the clubhouse, and this was no different.

"So, this is how you want to spend your twenty-first birthday?" Stella asked.

I smiled, "Yeah."

Stella sighed, "Ugh, we could go dancing at a club. Why, Co? Why?"

I giggled, "Do you remember what happened the last time we went to a club?" I asked her.

Her face paled, "Yeah, forget I said anything. This works. Totally works."

We went to a club when we were twenty to celebrate her cosmetology degree and my accounting degree.

Since we went to community college, it was easier for both of us.

But back to that night.

We had dressed up in short black dresses.

The night had been good.

We had gotten ready together at her house.

Stopped and had food, and then went to the club called Juice.

We had danced, and any time a guy tried to dance with us, we shoved them away.

Until one of the guys didn't appreciate it.

Oh, he had walked away...

Unbeknownst to us... we had someone watching us, making sure we stayed safe.

Pagan was there.

And over the years, Pagan had bulked up. And he had bulked up huge.

He wasn't as big as Creature... he just didn't have the height.

But he was as big as Coal.

Apparently, Pagan had read the situation correctly.

So, when the douchebag brought back four of his buddies... Pagan wasn't alone.

No.

Asher, Rome, and Stoney were there.

And when one of the frat boys looked at me and then looked at the brothers and asked, "How much?"

Asher lifted a brow, "Come again?"

"They must be y'all's whores. How much for the night?" The second douchebag asked.

Asher crossed his arms over his chest, "Which one are you asking about?"

"The dark one," the second douchebag said.

"That right?" Asher asked.

"Yeah, man. She's got a banging body."

"Well, for you going after her... afraid there isn't an amount I'd be willing to accept. Matter of fact... I'm going to give you to the count of five to get the fuck out of this club."

The third douchebag jerked his chin up, "And if we don't?"

"Then the five of you won't be leaving on your own two feet."

They all laughed. The fourth douchebag snickered, "There's five of us and three of you."

Asher lifted a shoulder, "Been far more than that against us. One."

They all snickered, then popped their knuckles and cracked their necks.

Then Asher said, "Two."

And when Asher got to five, Asher moved.

He wrapped his hand around one of the man's throats and forcibly shoved him out the door.

Rome knocked the second and third one out, then grabbed them by their legs and dragged them out the door.

Stoney moved then and grabbed the fourth guy by the back of his shirt and started to drag him out.

Pagan moved to the last guy and punched him in the face, then he, too, dragged the last guy out.

I looked at Stella, and then we both started laughing as we walked out of the club.

"That was hilarious." Stella snickered.

Asher stepped into the media room then and asked, "What was hilarious?"

Stella snickered again, then told him, "That time we went to the club... y'all dragging them out of there, then beating the dog shit out of them."

"That was fun," he said.

Then he looked at me, "What do you want for your birthday?"

I lifted a brow at him, "You already got me something."

And he had... he had gotten me a beautiful bracelet that matched my necklace perfectly.

He shrugged, "Name something I can do right now."

I looked at Stella, then thought about it... and said what the heck.

"I could do with a good foot massage and having my toes painted."

He nodded, and I kid you not, left, then returned half an hour later with a bag of stuff.

Stella left the room when he did and said she needed to get something from the kitchen.

"Prop your feet up for me," he said.

I didn't hesitate. They made a *thunk* sound when they landed on the black coffee table in front of the couch.

Which caused him to chuckle.

The media room consisted of three couches and two love seats, with end tables and two coffee tables.

It even had a popcorn machine as well as a soda fountain. I loved this room.

I watched as Asher sat down on the coffee table, then grabbed my feet and placed them in his lap.

Then he grinned and muttered, "Of course, you would have cute fucking toes."

How in the world did this man do this to me all the time?

Just by the words that fell from his mouth.

Because once again, my breath caught.

"My toes?" I asked after I got my breath going again.

He looked up at me and nodded.

Then, in a voice I hadn't heard from him before, something deep and raspy and full of... what exactly... "Yeah."

Then he proceeded to take out a bottle of lotion and a foot scrubber and got to work.

And when he massaged the soles of my feet, I let out a moan, which caused him to freeze for a split second, and if I hadn't had my eyes on his face, I would have missed the tick in his jaw, the vein throbbing in this neck, and the long exhale of breath.

Once he was finished, he pulled out four bottles of nail polish.

Pink. Red. Purple. Black.

He lifted them and lifted a brow, I smiled, "You pick."

He winked at me, then sat them all down but the red.

A deep red.

A deep red that was almost the same color as my prom dress.

Then, I watched as he proceeded to paint my toes perfectly.

And when I saw all of that, I asked, "You've had to have done this before with Stella."

He shook his head, then glanced up at me, "No. I didn't."

Then who has he done this for?

I've never been what you would call a jealous person.

Unless it was about eight years ago, and I watched Asher take one of the club girls' hands and lead her down the hall where the club girls stayed.

But I felt the jealousy growing, and somehow, Asher being Asher, he picked up on it, and how he knew it, I couldn't tell you.

"You're the first person I've done this for, Chloe. And I want it to look good."

What could I say to that and not mess up my friendship with Stella?

Honestly.

See... this was why I decided to distance myself from not only the club but from him.

Because seeing him as often as I did and knowing he couldn't be mine?

It was torture.

Pure freaking torture.

So, I did the only thing I could do: I nodded and said, "Well, thank you."

He winked, then put everything back in the back, and once he was done, he leaned forward and said, "Want to tell you something, and I need you to hear me, alright?"

I tilted my head to the side and nodded.

Then he whispered, "Meant what I said to you, Chloe. I'm going to wait. Just need you to tell me when you're ready. Because a connection like the two of us have is rare. And no way in fucking hell am I going to go to my grave and not know what it feels like to have all of you."

The only thing I could ask him was, "All of me?"

He nodded, "Yeah. I want your body. I want your mind. But most of all, I want your heart. I want to plant myself so deep inside of it that it will take you a millennium to dig me out."

And before I could say anything... like... Stella.

There was a tap in the doorway.

Asher and I both looked in the direction and saw Priest standing there, "Sorry to interrupt. But I fucking need you, Asher."

I looked back at Asher and saw him visibly sigh, then lift his chin.

He looked back at me, apology brimming in his toffee-colored eyes, then he carefully removed my feet from his lap, stood, leaned forward, wrapped his hand around the side of my neck, pressed his lips to my forehead, and there he whispered, "Remember what I said, alright?"

All I managed to do was let out a clipped nod.

Yes, I watched him as he walked away, but he stopped in the doorway, turned, and asked, "Did you know that my favorite color is red?"

I nodded, then without a filter, I said, "Yeah. You wear it a lot. And you have red accents on your bike."

And with that, he walked away.

Stella returned a few minutes after he left, sat down beside me, took in my toes, grinned, and then asked, "So, what did y'all talk about?"

I shrugged, "The usual."

Thankfully, she let it go and got back into the movie we had been watching.

But for the remainder of the night, I replayed his words over and over in my head.

Dark-haired.

Green-eyed.

Beauties.

I will wait for you.

But most of all, I want your heart. I want to plant myself so deep inside of it that it will take you a millennium to dig me out.

Oh, what was I going to do?

I knew to move across the country.

How much would that cost?

Probably a lot.

Definitely more than I had in my bank account.

But... maybe... maybe Stella would be okay with it.

I mean, she did leave the room when he came in here.

She never said a word about me and her dad texting.

She knew about it.

Sometimes, she would even ask me about it.

.... I just didn't know how to go about any of this without someone getting hurt.

And my mama was right.

Like she always is.

I think the greatest harm anyone can do to themselves is to deny what the heart wants. No one wants to be miserable.

Chapter 8

Asher – Present – Age 42

Looking at the applications of club girls, the brothers and I looked at each one of them and then passed it on.

We had seventy-four applications.

Seventy-four.

That was the most this club had ever seen.

We usually kept between four to five club girls.

But with Pipe claiming Gabby. Coal claiming Adeline. And Irish is pulling his head from his ass about Sutton. We were out of three girls.

Right now, we had Lizette.

And that was it. And she was getting tired. The brothers deserved something new.

Three club girls stood out to the brothers.

Kayla. Flo. Hanna.

When I saw on Flo's application that she was a club girl for the Dogwood charter of Wrath MC, I tagged my phone and called Powers.

Then, once he answered on the third ring, I put it on speaker.

"Asher. Long time. How's it going?" I heard his woman, Lil, obliviously telling their two kids to clean up their breakfast plates.

I chuckled at the mom voice she had used, then I said, "It's fucking going. But got a question for you."

Powers's tone was serious when he said, "Ask."

"We need club girls. We're down three. Got one in front of me. Said she used to be one of y'all's."

"Name?" he asked.

"Flo." And if the woman wasn't a bitch, that was a cool name.

Powers chuckled then and said, "Well, fuck."

That caused something in my gut to tighten, I asked, "Well fuck what?"

He chuckled again, "Been wondering where she went off to."

I lifted a brow, "She trouble?"

He hesitated for a moment, then asked, "Y'all got a bunch of ol' ladies?"

It was my turn to hesitate for a moment on how to answer him.

I locked eyes with Priest.

He never made his wife his ol' lady, and I knew he was glad that he hadn't. Because after she served him with divorce papers and wanted to trade him in for someone with more money, I never wanted to see that bitch again.

And I knew that if Priest ever met another woman that he showed interest in, she was going to have to be patient.

And I mean patient as fuck.

But we had Gabby, Adeline, and finally Sutton.

Gabby was Pipe's ol' lady.

Adeline was Coal's ol' lady.

Sutton was Irish's ol' lady.

And as for me... well... I didn't want to get into that at the moment.

I said, "We got three ol' ladies."

"They the type to let it known that they won't tolerate anyone hitting on their men?" Powers asked.

I looked at Pipe, Coal, and Irish.

And all at once, they grinned.

I chuckled, "Oh yeah."

"Then you shouldn't have anything to worry about. But a word of advice, make it clear to her that if a brother has an ol' lady, and she messes with that, she's out on her ass. And don't be lenient with that shit. Cause you give that bitch an inch, she'll take a fucking mile."

After we hung up, we voted.

And we voted for Kayla, Flo, and Hanna.

There was one more matter to vote on, and I told Ivan I would bring it to the table.

"I got a visit a few months ago. Then we talked it over." I locked eyes with Rome. "This is your call; it's up to you. Ivan Svankov is stepping down as the mafia's cleaner. He's retiring and wants to spend time with his wife and daughter."

Rome jerked up his chin, "Heard about that. Word is he's reached out to you and two others."

I lifted a brow, "Who?"

"A man he knew way back in Russia. Sergei Alekseev, he's the Sovietnik for Maksim Kostikov. And the other, he's the Sovietnik for Konstantin Mikhailov."

I leaned back in my chair and thought it over. It was a good plan. With Maksim, the new Pakhan of the east of the United States, and Konstantin, the new Pakhan of the north, a lot more ground will be covered. I liked it. It was a damn good plan.

But... "You gotta think on it. It's a big undertaking. Not sure your woman will be okay with it."

Rome lifted his chin, "I'll talk to her about it."

And he would because there wasn't a move Rome made unless he talked it over with Collins. She wasn't his ol' lady. But we all knew he was hers.

"Anything else that needs to be brought to the table?" I asked.

And when no one opened their mouths, I slammed the gavel on the table.

It was time to get the clubhouse ready for the party we were hosting this weekend.

***

That night, as I lay in my bed behind my closed eyelids, I allowed myself the one pleasure I had given myself.

She was old enough now.

It wasn't criminal.

Some might say it was criminal to have done what I did.

But I knew that at the end of the day, as long as she ended the day in my bed, then I didn't consider any of it not to be worth it.

I would do it all over again for it to be her face I saw at the end of the day and the first thing I saw every morning.

Perhaps that was why, after four hours of lying in bed awake, I had gotten up, dressed, then got on my bike and rode to where I did.

And, like always... her bedroom window was open.

Chapter 9

Chloe – Present – Age 21

I had been waiting for this.

Needing this.

For years and years and freaking years.

I wanted to pinch myself.

Because this had better be real life.

If I found out this was a dream... there was no telling what I would do.

My eyes stared at his amazing body. Fit. Tattooed. Sprinkles of grey on his chest.

Even though the man was twenty-one years older than I was... it didn't make me see any less in him.

It just meant he was put on this earth well before I was so he could learn how to pleasure me in all ways.

And boy, he did that in spades.

My hands were running through that soft black hair with sprinkles of gray in it.

My nails were scraping along his shoulders, down his back as he moved his body lower.

Muscles rippling.

Veins popping.

The feel of his mouth on my most private area.

No one has gone near the area unless it was my parents when I was a baby or the female doctor.

His tongue weaving a spell over my clit.

Wanting more.

Needing more.

His body came up, sliding all that hardness over my sensitized skin.

Pressing a kiss where my heart lay, he whispered, "I love you, Chloe."

I smiled, "I love you too, Asher.

His head lowered, his lips brushing against mine.

My body was on fire.

Needing him.

Craving him.

Finally.

Finally, we were going to connect as one.

Then, just as he moved to enter me...

Beep. Beep. Beep. Beep.

My eyes opened, and I sat up, my body was covered in a sheen of sweat.

My tank top and shorts were sticking to my body.

And what was worse than all of that, my fingers were in my cotton sleep shorts.

Jerking my hand out of my shorts, I closed my eyes, slapped the alarm clock, and collapsed back into bed.

I relished the soft breeze that blew in through my open window. I knew it was a bad habit that anyone could climb in through, but we all must go some time, I might as well sleep comfortably.

Then I heard my mama's voice through the door. "Mija, love, it's time to get up. It's time for work."

I sighed, "Yeah, Mama."

I took in a deep breath and then let it out.

Why?

Why couldn't I just live in my dreams?

Was there a way to make that happen?

You know, like in *Charmed* and the episode called the *Dream Sorcerer*.

But I don't want to die in the dream.

Ugh... why couldn't I be a witch?

My phone beeped with a message.

Knowing who it was, I felt like the crappiest friend that was ever born.

Stella and I had become friends in the second grade.

Some mean girls had been picking on her for wearing black motorcycle boots and having her hair all wild.

Honestly, I thought she looked like the coolest kid I had ever seen.

And when I heard them calling her biker trash, biker whore, and stroker girl, I had gotten mad.

And seeing as I had my daddy's temper and my mamma's temper, it wouldn't go well for those two girls.

I took the persona of a *Señora del Fuego* when my temper was riled.

Fire lady. I loved calling myself that.

See, my daddy was third-generation Irish, and my mama was a fourth-generation Mexican American.

I looked like my mama.

Soft, dark brown hair, tanned skin, button nose, short stature, curves in all the right places.

And the only thing of my daddy's... his eyes. Green. But not just any color of green, it was a cross between sage and the brightest emerald. The most perfect color ever created if you wanted my opinion on the matter.

So, when you combine my mama and my daddy, I have a temper that can rival a sailor.

That was why I climbed down the monkey bars, clenched my fists, and stormed over to the girls.

Without thinking, I shoved myself bodily in between them and then got into their faces.

My Spanish was in full force as I said, *"Lleva tu maldad a otra parte. Eres una bruja fea."*

The ring leader, Veronica, opened her mouth to say something, but that was when one of the teachers walked over and said, "Okay, okay. Let's break it up."

I looked up at her and snapped, "You should have been over here breaking it up instead of messing with your phone." And she had been. I had watched her.

She looked at me and snapped back, "Go to the office. Now." I nodded, then turned to look at the girl.

I held out my hand to her and said, "I'm Chloe. You are?"

She smiled, placed her hand in mine, and shook it once, twice, then said, "Hi, Chloe. I'm Stella. What did you say?"

I grinned, ignoring the teacher who was getting irritated with me, and said, "I told her to take your nastiness somewhere else. And I called her an ugly witch."

I had gone to the office to wait on my mama.

When she got there, she calmly asked me what had happened, and I told her.

She smiled once I was done and then took me for ice cream.

But it was nothing that compared to getting home afterward to see a big black motorcycle with hints of red in the driveway, a man atop it, with Stella behind him.

And it was nothing compared to him smiling at me while saying thank you.

And like that, my little heart had been captured.

But...that was that.

Stella and my bond had been forever cemented on the playground.

But now... I didn't know how I was going to face Stella and, for that matter, Asher.

Gah.

My mama knocked on my door again, "Mi hija, time to get up."

I needed to move out.

Unfortunately, I was paying off my college loans, and it was smart to stay with my parents rent-free while I did that.

Six more months. Six more months, and I would be able to do that.

Sighing, I rolled out of bed, showered, and got ready for the day.

As I took a sip of my coffee, coffee that looked like a white piece of paper, I texted Stella back.

Stella – *Don't forget. We both offered to help with the food this weekend at the clubhouse.*

Me – *I haven't forgotten. I'll be making Tamales and Blueberry salad.*

Stella – *Dad wants to know if you're also making that marbled tres leches cake.*

Dang it.

She had to bring up her dad.

I so didn't need that right now.

Not after the dream I had.

Oh hell, who was I kidding?

That man was on my mind almost every second of every day.

But alas, I was a big girl.

Which was why I texted back.

Me – *Have him buy the stuff. I'm already maxed out this month.*

And I was. I couldn't afford anything else until my next paycheck hit at the end of next week.

Stella – *K. Have a good day at work. Love you, snookums.*

I shook my head.

Me – *You too. Don't fry anyone's hair.*

Asher being Asher, he didn't buy the stuff.

No, what he did do was run by my work and drop off two crisp one-hundred-dollar bills.

And when I tried to refuse the cash and ask him if he had a fifty, he lifted a brow while saying, "You shouldn't be paying for shit to feed the brothers."

That was also how a couple of the women I worked with developed crushes on him.

Asher on his bike, the sun just right... I wanted a picture of that.

Jesus, but I was such a sucker for this man.

Perhaps it was time for me to find someone else and try to forget about my stupid, unrequited crush on him.

Stella. Stella. Stella.

I repeated her name over and over in my head.

But... the thought of even being in the same vicinity as someone else who wasn't Asher made my heart physically ache.

What the heck was I going to do?

How in the world did someone uncreate feelings for another person when they had secretly loved that person before they knew what the word *love* actually meant?

Chapter 10

Asher – Present – Age 42

Today had been one thing after another.

We were trying to develop a new route to deliver guns, and one thing after another was wrong with every single route.

I knew that I was growing more grey hairs atop my head and in my beard.

Something had to fucking give.

That was why I slammed my fist down on the table we had in church, locked my eyes on Irish, and said, "Figure this fucking shit out. Pick a goddamned route already. Enough is e-fucking-nough."

He nodded, "Got it, Pres. Sorry. Maisie has been having these weird dreams about that bitch abandoning her again."

I nodded, "I got it." I said, then swept my hand through my hair and said, "You need anything? Just gotta let me know, yeah?"

He jerked his chin.

Looking at the brothers, I said, "Alright, enough fucking heavy shit. Let's go eat and get drunk."

Trigger laughed, "And get laid."

Once I banged the gavel on the table, we all stood up and walked out of the room.

The smells of great food wafted from the kitchen.

Tagging my phone, I pulled it out, knowing it had vibrated a few times.

One of them was from a woman I had a friends-with-benefits thing going on for a bit when Stella was younger.

Word got around that she got married and then divorced again.

Word also got around that she was the one to divorce him.

But I knew better, and I had found out.

He had divorced her because she couldn't keep her legs closed.

April – *Hey, Asher. Been thinking about you lately. I could use your massive cock right now. I need to blow off some steam.*

And below that was a picture.

I didn't even bother to look at it, it was either her tits, which weren't all that great, or it was a shot of her pussy.

It wasn't that I wasn't interested in getting laid, April was a sure thing.

But... just the thought of letting another woman touch me who wasn't a certain someone caused my balls to shrivel up.

That was probably why I exited that text thread, went to her number, and blocked it.

Another text was there from Powers.

Powers – *Got a dove coming to y'all. Be there late next week.*

Me – *Got it. We'll be ready.*

Me – *Status?*

While I waited for him to text me back, I looked at the other messages.

Declan – *This motherfucker happens to venture into your area, show him what's what.*

I studied the picture.

Me – *What did the fucker do?*

Declan – *Thought it would be hilarious to stick a sign that read 'retarded' on Chelsea's back at school today.*

I nodded, then sent the picture in a group chat, telling them to keep their eyes peeled.

Me – *Got it.*

My phone vibrated in my hand.

Powers – *8.*

That meant that the woman had gotten the hell beaten out of her, and the court system had failed her. Utterly. Rat bastards.

Princess – *I'm running late.*

Princess – *Shit. No, I'm not. I'm good.*

Princess – *You must be in church. Come find me when you're done. Love you.*

I couldn't help but snicker at my girl.

Chloe – *Total was $47.98. Got your change.*

I shook my head at that girl.

If I ever heard of anyone calling Chloe a gold-digger, I was knocking their teeth down their throat.

Me – *Keep the change, Chloe.*

Chloe – *Asher, that's not right. I really don't mind.*

Me – *Chloe, I know you're independent. Admire it. But. Keep. The. Fucking. Cash.*

Chloe – *Okay. Fine. Thank you. There was a new pair of shorts that caught my eye.*

Me – *Bring me the change.*

That was when I heard her tinkling laughter, and when I looked up, it was to see her pocketing her phone as she carried a dish outside.

The party went off without a hitch.

Beer. Whiskey. Moonshine. You name it, we had it. It flowed into everyone's cups.

The food was fucking perfect.

And I may or may not have eaten a little bit of the food.

Only to leave plenty of fucking room for the food that Chloe made.

And that was why I was sitting here, beside Stella, watching as Chloe gathered her trash and stood, then walked over to the trash can.

It hadn't gone unnoticed that she barely talked to Stella or me the entire time we ate.

And it also hadn't gone unnoticed that the smiles she was usually so frequent to give were hard to pull out.

Once Chloe was far enough away, I looked at Stella, "Chloe, alright?"

She nodded, "Yeah, why?"

"Don't know. Something ain't right." I said as I watched Chloe move around the courtyard, moving the empty dishes and making room for more.

Stella looked away from me, then at Chloe, and said, "She said she had a good day at work, so I don't know. But she has seemed kind of off. I'll go talk to her."

I shook my head, "Nah. I got it. You need to finish those videos on that technique you've been trying to nail."

She grinned, "Are you going to let me practice on the boys?"

I stood up and looked down at her, "You want to be visiting me through a plate glass window while I wear nothing but orange because one of them accidentally touched you?"

She giggled, then shook her head, "Nope."

I tapped her nose, "Didn't fucking think so."

Being the kind of man I was... I didn't delay in walking over to where Chloe was moving the dishes around to make room for more.

Because even though everyone had finished eating, give it half an hour and the food would be attacked once again.

The moment I reached her, my hand snaked out and curled around her bicep.

Electric shocks went up my arm.

Her head whipped around, and for a moment, her gaze softened... then... in the blink of an eye, it was gone, and her expression became guarded.

What the fuck?

That caused me to lift my brow and ask, "Chloe, everything okay?"

She nodded, "Yeah, Pres. All good."

I lifted a brow at her, "Didn't know you were a brother." I teased.

Usually, she would smile at that.

But she didn't.

"Since when did I stop being Asher to you?" I asked her.

It had taken years, and I mean fucking years, for her to stop calling me Mr. Hendrix.

She shrugged.

Oh no. That wouldn't fucking do.

"Chloe, what's going on?" I asked.

My eyes stared intently down into hers.

For the briefest of moments, her cheeks pinkened.

Then she looked away, and in a soft voice I had to strain to hear, she said, "It's nothing. Please, let it go."

Like fuck. I wouldn't let a goddamned thing go when it came to her, "Chloe..."

"Pres. Phone call." I heard Whit say.

I squeezed her bicep gently, then said, "Chloe, talk to me."

She shook her head, her eyes coming to mine for a minute, then flickering away, "You need to answer that call, Pres."

I bit back a growl at her calling me that a-fucking-gain.

"Chloe," I said.

She didn't look up at me. She just stood there staring down at the tops of her shoes.

What I wouldn't give to have the fucking right to place my fingertip underneath her chin, and lift her head, cause fuck, but I wanted to see those mesmerizing green eyes of hers.

It almost felt as though my day didn't start unless I got a look at those beauties.

Perhaps that was why I had cropped a picture of her and Stella when they were both eighteen.

I cropped it so the only thing I saw was Chloe's eyes.

Sighing, when she still didn't look at me nor speak, I said, "I'll stand here all goddamned day until you tell me what's wrong. You don't tell me; I can't fucking fix it."

"Asher. Phone, brother." Whit was at my side now.

Not taking my eyes off Chloe, I said, "I'll call whoever it is back."

Whit started to say, "Ash..."

"Whit. Go. The. Fuck. Away." I growled.

My eyes never once left Chloe's face.

Fuck, but what I wouldn't give to throw her over my shoulder and carry her to my office, press her body into the wall, and feel all that softness pressed to my hard body.

But she wasn't ready for that.

And we weren't there.

Yet.

"Pres. It's nothing. Okay. Please. Just let it go." She said, her temper starting to get the best of her.

She tried to take her arm from my hand, but I held on, still gently, because I would be damned if I ever caused a bruise to form on her skin.

She growled like a cute little tiger cub. Fuck. Me.

And when I didn't move nor let go of the hold I had on her, her head shot up, her sage green eyes sparking with fire.

"I asked you to let it go. Jesus Christ, can't I process things in my own dang time?" She snapped.

I hid the grin.

Because I fucking loved when she let her temper loose.

It wasn't that often, and that was a goddamned shame.

But... then again... maybe it wasn't.

Because I didn't want anyone else to see this side of her.

On a bad day, Chloe was a thirteen.

On a good day, she was a twenty-six.

And when her temper was unleashed, that woman was a fucking sixty-eight.

"It's none of your business. You're not related to me. You're not fucking me. Therefore, I don't owe you a freaking thing." And with that, she tore her arm from my grasp and stomped away from me.

While all that was taking place, Whit came over to my side, "I ever spoke to you that way, you'd chop my balls off."

I didn't take my eyes off Chloe's retreating form when I said, "Then feed them down your throat."

Stella came over to my side and asked, "What happened? The last time she stormed away from you, you had berated her for wearing those short shorts. Even though it was closing in on a hundred and five degrees that day."

I shook my head at her, "No clue. She wouldn't tell me."

And with that, I walked away and headed to my office to do something that I had no business in doing.

Yes, I had gotten hard when I saw Chloe after I exited church.

And yes, I had stayed hard while we ate.

But I had become rock fucking hard after she flashed that temper at me and then stormed away.

Her hips swayed with every stomp.

Fuck me, but I wanted to take a bite out of her ass.

The moment the door closed behind me, I threw the lock.

Undoing my belt, my button, my fly, I pulled my dick from its confines, wrapped my hand around it, gripped it hard, and then started to stroke.

And all I had to bring to focus was that fucking blush of hers.

I came faster than a virgin kid who was being laid by the top-rated porn star in the nation.

My head was resting against the door as I tried to calm my breathing.

If I came that hard from a hand job from my own fucking hand, how would it feel when I finally thrust my cock into her welcoming heat?

I know... I needed to have a plot picked out and my headstone at the ready.

It was hours later after I cleaned myself up and my mess, that I was sitting in my office chair once I knocked out some paperwork and called Marquez back on an order he wanted to place for weapons and ammo.

That fucking blush.

I couldn't get it off my mind.

And what was more were the words she had spoken to me.

'It's none of your business. You're not related to me. You're not fucking me. Therefore, I don't owe you a freaking thing.'

I sat back in my chair, taking a puff off the cigar.

It was a special moment.

The second special moment in my life.

But I had a decision to make.

However, before I made that decision, there was someone I needed to find because I would be damned if I put Chloe through that.

But just like everything regarding Chloe, I didn't know if I could do that.

And my decision?

I told her I would wait for her.

And I fucking would.

But she didn't grasp how deep my feelings ran for her.

I had told her a few things that would clue her in... but I didn't know if I could spend the rest of my days watching her from afar, keeping her safe.... but I knew that I would.

If my feelings weren't returned, that was exactly what I would be doing.

All I needed was the smallest chance that her heart knew what it truly felt for me.

All he needed was one spark from her.

I could work on the rest.

After all, she was the one who started that spark in me. I wasn't fucking her.

I'd done a lot of things in his life.

Taken a lot of lives.

And none of them I regretted.

But I knew that nothing in my life, so far, would ever be as hard as fighting for the one woman who was the other part of my soul.

Good thing I was ready for the fight.

And with that, I took one more puff from my cigar and fucking smiled.

Chloe

I knew Asher wouldn't let me get away with not answering him.

And I hated how smart he was.

But then again, it was one of the things I adored about him.

But I couldn't tell him about the dream I had a few days ago and everything it entailed.

I just couldn't.

I'd been secretly in love with that man for years. Almost a decade.

But... I loved Stella more.

She was the best friend a girl could ever ask for.

And there was nothing I would ever do to ruin that friendship.

After that dream, distancing myself wasn't going to work.

It hadn't been working.

And since I couldn't afford to move to the other side of the country... there was only one thing I could do...

Asher

I was fit to be tied.

Had I not gone the way I went, coming back to the clubhouse from grabbing a few things at the store, then I never would have seen what I did.

And I was seeing red.

And I knew everyone saw it.

They were all keeping a wide berth away from me.

Sitting in a chair at the corner table in the clubhouse, I kept my eyes trained on the door.

Waiting.

Because I knew that Stella and Chloe were on their way here.

How dare she allow another man to touch her?

How dare she allow another man in a breathable atmosphere.

Half an hour later, when the door finally opened and I saw her, I stood up and stormed over to her, and without a care, I asked, "Who was that man I saw you at the restaurant with?"

Stella froze while she was digging in her bag for something, and Chloe scrunched her brows, then she asked, "What man?"

And through gritted teeth, I said, "The man you were looking all cozy with at the Backyard Grill."

Chloe shook her head, then whispered, "I have no idea. Truly, who are you talking about?"

I snapped, "The fucking man in the black polo shirt. The fucking man who had his hand on your shoulder. The fucking man who smiled at you. And the fucking man you gave a certain smile to."

"Oh," she said in a hushed whisper and then did something I never thought she would do.

"Oh? Who the fuck was he, Chloe?" I asked.

And I wouldn't be asking her again.

One way or another, I was going to get the answer out of her.

And if it was what I suspected... then I was going to hunt the bastard down and rip his hand from his body.

The same hand he had used to touch the one person who was untouchable unless it was by me.

And when she opened her mouth and said the words she had, *I was on a date...* I had no choice.

Fuck.

I was adding another black mark to my soul.

And I didn't care. Not one single fucking bit.

Chapter 11

Chloe

Two weeks later, I didn't say anything when the guy I had been on a date with, Jacob, Jared, John, something that started with a J, had completely ghosted me.

Because the entire date, everything had felt wrong.

The way he held his fork.

The way he drank his drink.

The way his eyes moved to other women.

Everything.

And I knew why... it was because he wasn't *him*.

I was screwed.

So, freaking screwed.

I sighed as I folded the last piece of laundry and put it in the drawer.

And when I turned away from the dresser, something caught my attention.

Was that a creak on the stairs?

That was odd.

My parents were out on their weekly date night.

But before I could make a move away from the spot I was in, something all in black burst through my door.

And before I could scream, a hand was clamped over my mouth.

My body was turned and pressed against my dresser.

Hands.

Hands that felt so wrong were grabbing me.

I tried to move my lips to scream.

I tried to move my mouth to bite on the hand that was still over my mouth.

My body bucked, trying to dislodge whoever it was behind me.

My hands swung widely, trying to hit whoever it was.

And when a hand moved to the waistband of my sleep shorts, I had never felt more grateful when my hand closed around a heavy candle stick holder I had on my dresser.

I grabbed it and then swung up and back.

The sound of something hard smacking flesh and bone reverberated around my room.

And when those hands let go of me, the body moved back, I spun and then hit the person in the face with the candle stick holder as hard as I could.

The person had on a black mask over his face, but there was no mistaking his eyes.

Eyes I had seen before.

But I wasn't going to be one of those women who hesitated. You hesitate, and you get hurt.

Therefore, while the man was disoriented, I raced around, grabbed my phone, and flew down the stairs.

The moment I made it to the front door, I saw the deadbolt was locked.

As my shaking fingers unlocked it, I heard heavy footsteps racing down the stairs.

But I got that door unlocked, opened, and then... I ran.

I ran for so long that I wasn't sure where I was.

I ran for so long that I felt a hitch in my side.

And then I power-walked until I got to something familiar.

Seeing the diner on the corner, I raced into it.

Eyes came to me, but I paid them no attention.

I brought up my phone, winced when I saw it was at seven percent, and then I placed a call.

My hands were shaking as I brought the phone to my ear.

A waitress started to make her way over to me, but she slowed when she took in my appearance.

I breathed out a sigh of relief when I heard, "Chloe?"

Then he shouted, his voice laced with anger, "You better get back, you sorry piece of shit."

"Asher?" I couldn't stop the tremble in my voice.

The immediate anger she had heard had disappeared immediately. "Chloe?"

With tears I hadn't realized were spilling down my cheeks, I asked, "Can... you come... and g... get me?"

He was silent for a beat. Only a beat, then I heard, "Fuck this shit." And then I heard a gunshot, which was immediately followed by, "Where are you?"

"The diner on the corner of Seventh and Main."

"Okay. Be there in ten minutes." And with that, I heard running and then the sound of motorcycles coming to life.

He was breathing heavily when he said, "I gotta let you go so I can get to you. But are you safe?"

I looked down at my bare feet, wiped the tears from my eyes, and nodded, "Yeah, I think so."

"Okay, Doll Baby, be there in ten. Just hang on for me. And Chloe, whatever you need to do to keep breathing, you fucking do it. Do you understand me?"

I nodded, "Yeah, Asher."

And with that, he hung up.

Pulling the phone from my ear, the woman who had approached me looked to be a few years older than me, and when I read her nametag, it read *Leighton*.

"Are you okay, hon?" She had stunning red hair that was tied back in a braid and the bluest eyes I had ever seen.

I almost wanted to ask her if they were contacts.

But after everything that had happened, I just didn't think I had it in me. Instead, I shook my head, "No. But I will be.'

She nodded, smiled softly, then asked, "Do you need me to call the cops?"

I shook my head, "No. I have someone on the way. But thank you."

She nodded, "Okay, well, how about we get you up on a stool and a cup of coffee? Your feet look a mess."

I nodded, gratefully.

With a warm cup of coffee in my hands, I kept my eyes trained on the door, making sure I didn't see him.

After I inhaled a much-needed breath, that was when I felt it.

The rumble from the motorcycles made the ground shake beneath her feet.

There, in the distance, she saw the headlights.

Uncaring what people were going to say. I wanted to feel safe. And that safety only came with one man.

On the back of that monster bike, there he sat.

I watched as he almost laid his bike down when he brought it to a stop. He was off it and storming toward the diner.

And the moment he opened the door, I carelessly placed the cup of coffee on the counter, dropped to my feet, and winced at the pain, but I didn't care.

I took off, and when I saw that Asher had luckily braced himself and held his arms out, the moment I reached him, I flung myself into his body.

His arms closed around me as he pulled me into his chest.

His familiar scent of smoke and cedar caused even more tears to pour down my cheeks.

Because it meant one thing.

I was safe.

I buried my nose in his neck, inhaling the scent of safety and home.

Once my tears were done, Asher pulled his neck back, then bent it down to take in my features.

Then his gaze moved lower, and I knew he saw my feet.

Without a word, he shrugged off his kutte, handed it to me, and then pulled the black hoodie he was wearing and helped me in it.

Only when he had his kutte back on did he pick me up carefully and carry me to his bike.

Once he sat me down, he placed two fingers underneath my chin and lifted my face up until my eyes locked with his.

"Who?" he asked.

Was it really fire I saw burning in his hazel eyes, and when I saw how hard his face was, I knew that I wasn't imagining things.

Therefore, I said the only thing I could, "My dad's best friend. Marco Rubina."

Out of the corner of my eye, I saw Whit take his phone out and place a call.

"What happened?" he asked.

I took in the passerby and whispered, "Wouldn't it be better to tell you all of this at the clubhouse?"

He shook his head, "Normally, it would. But with you, I need all the details."

I nodded, "Mom and Dad went out for their weekly date night. I was putting laundry away. And that was when I heard a creak on the staircase. Before I could make a move, a figure all clad in black rushed into my bedroom. He had his hand over my mouth, my front pressed to my dresser. And when I felt his hand at the waistband of my shorts, I grabbed a heavy candlestick holder and hit him with it. Then I hit him again, grabbed my phone, and ran. Then, when I got here, I called you."

He nodded, then swallowed, and that tick was in his jaw, as well as that vein in his neck was throbbing.

Then it seemed he got control of himself, and he said softly, "Okay. Thank you. Want us to go to your house to see if he's there?"

I shook my head, "No, he probably isn't."

He nodded, "Okay, here's what's going to happen. I'm going to take you to the clubhouse, and you're going to call your parents and Stella. Then we'll get your feet looked at. Okay?"

I nodded.

And that was that.

But as I turned my head, I saw that the entire motorcycle club was there, and Rome, Creature, Pagan, Stoney, Priest, and Coal all had specs of blood on their arms or faces.

I looked back at Asher, who was pulling a helmet out of his saddlebags, "Did I interrupt something important?"

He looked at me as he handed me the helmet, then helped me strap it on, and only once it was secured, he said, "Nothing is more important than you. Fucking nothing."

Then he moved, climbed in front of me, and started the bike.

The rumble filled the night sky.

As soon as I was curled tight to his back, we headed to the clubhouse.

I called my mama, and she and my dad were on the way to the clubhouse.

Then I called Stella.

She beat my parents to the clubhouse.

And was smothering me in a hug.

She only released me when my mama did the same thing and then my dad.

And when I told them all what happened, I said, "I recognized his eyes."

My mama snarled, "Who was that pendejo?"

I looked up at my dad and smiled a sad smile.

He picked up on it and said, "I'm not going to like this. Am I?"

I shook my head, "It was Marco, Dad."

He was silent for a beat.

Then he turned and punched the wall.

"I'm going to kill that lying sack of trash. He told me he had changed. That he saw the light. And I'm the dumb motherfucker that allowed him to be in the same house where my daughter sleeps."

Asher growled from behind him, "You're going to have to get in line."

My dad turned and looked at Asher.

I couldn't make out that look.

But after a minute or two, my dad nodded.

Umm... okay.

"We've got people looking for him. We'll have him before the sun comes up." Asher said with one hundred percent honesty.

That made me shiver, but I felt no remorse for what was about to happen to him.

He had creeped me out for years.

And when I told Asher that after he carried me to his bedroom to clean my feet, he wanted to know why I hadn't told him.

"Because I only saw him a handful of times. And you have enough on your plate without worrying about some creepy guy."

He sighed, then ran his hand through his hair, "I want to know about everything that involves you, Chloe. How many times do I need to make that clear?"

I didn't have a chance to answer him because he started cleaning my feet.

And all with a gentle hand.

How in the world could the president of an outlaw motorcycle club have gentle hands?

I knew the answer.

Because he was Asher.

And he could do anything.

In thinking that, I closed my eyes and didn't realize I had fallen asleep.

Asher

I didn't know how long I sat there after I had cleaned up her feet.

Minutes?

Hours?

I wasn't sure.

But a few things were running on a loop in my head.

It took some motherfucker trying to rape her before I got her in my bed.

I was going to send him a thank you card in hell.

Because you can bet your fucking ass that I will be sending that motherfucker to hell in a few short hours.

Damn, but she looked good in my bed.

Her tanned skin against my white sheets. Her dark hair fanned out over my pillow.

A soft knock came at the door.

I stood up, stretched, and headed to it.

When I opened it, it was to see Trigger with a grin on his face. "Found him."

Stella moved around Trigger and said, "I'm staying with Chloe."

I kissed her cheek, then moved to the side and watched as my daughter carefully climbed into my bed and got beside Chloe.

It didn't hit me then that Stella never said a word about how I was with Chloe.

And it wouldn't hit me until a week later.

I looked at Trigger and nodded, "Let's go."

Forty-five minutes later, we found him.

Right where Charlie said he would be.

And with my brothers at my back, I kicked the piece of shit's door open and grinned when I saw the damage my Doll Baby had done to his face.

Coal and Rome rushed him and had him pinned.

But it was Rome who was fixated on something on the man's pec.

And then he said, "Well, look what we have here."

I looked at it and couldn't help but smile. Huge.

"Well. Well. Well. It would seem we finally found you, you piece of shit."

There on the man's pec was none other than a pair of shackles with fire behind it and the words Verity Runners MC. But I knew he was who we had been looking for, that fucking five-point crown that was resting atop one of the flames.

His trademark.

I kept my promise to Chloe's father.

He didn't stay breathing when the sun came up.

He also had been beaten by every brother.

And for the pièce de resistance, the man had received cuts into his body for all the kids we found out about over the past couple of years he had trafficked.

Since he didn't deserve a fast death, not for this piece of shit, I did the only thing that felt right.

I pulled my knife from the middle of my back, placed my black-gloved hand over his forehead, held the bastard in place, and then I ran my knife over his throat.

When nothing but our heavy breathing filled the room and the scent of iron in the air, I smiled.

Then I watched as I sat on my bike with my brothers and smoked a cigar after we had gone through his monstrosity of a home while piles of cocaine, heroin, and meth went up in flames.

Our saddlebags were loaded down with cash we found.

We would be cleaning it.

And then making anonymous donations to all the kids we had recovered that he had trafficked.

As the sun peaked over the horizon, it was a good start to the day.

The moment I walked into the clubhouse with my brothers at my back, Chloe's dad stood up and met us.

He took us all in.

The blood on our shirts.

Our busted knuckles.

He held his hand up and offered it to me.

I shook it.

Then he clapped me on the back and said, "When you ask for her hand, I'll say yes."

He stepped to the side, and her mother was there.

She rose on her tiptoes and kissed my cheek, then she whispered, "Be mindful of her heart. And take my words to mind. Make sure no skeletons in your closet can hurt her. Because I promise you this: when she loves, she loves hard. And she won't hesitate to go down with you."

I took her words to heart.

I really did.

That was when I called Teague.

Teague was a member of Wrath MC, Texas chapter in Bradford Valley. He had connections that Charlie could only dream of having.

And I was done waiting.

Chloe

When Asher returned, he said I wouldn't have to worry about Marco.

And I believed him.

Even more so when I caught sight of him pulling his shirt over his head and throwing it in the trash can.

I wasn't going to comment on the view of that man shirtless.

Because if I did... well... I would need to be sprayed with a fire extinguisher.

He had muscles for days. And at his age, it was dang impressive.

And the tattoos. One's that spread from his pecs to his shoulders and over to his shoulder blades and down his arms... I wanted to lick every single line...

Stop it, Chloe, I silently berated myself.

Jesus Christ.

***

My father had apologized repeatedly, and honestly, I didn't blame him.

He didn't make Marco do all those things.

He didn't have a hand in what I now knew about Marco.

All those poor kids.

My heart wept for them.

But they would never know that Zagan MC took the man who was largely responsible out and sent him to hell.

But I knew.

And even though my bedroom felt like it was tainted, I still slept like a baby.

Asher

Chloe's mother's words came to mind as I hung up the phone with Teague.

I only had one skeleton in my closet, and it was split into two parts.

I now knew where to find her. I also found out how she's been able to avoid me for the past five years.

I just didn't expect *her* to find me before I had found *her*...

Chapter 12

Chloe

Three days later, the party at the clubhouse was in full force, and I had my hands thrown up in the air, I spun around, swinging my hips in time to the music.

There was just something about a slow rock song that fed the soul.

And I lived for it.

And I was glad that I got to live for it.

Had it not been for that candlestick holder, I stopped that train of thought.

And I was glad I had because just as I lowered my arms, I ran my hands through my hair, my eyes were closed, my hips swaying, when I suddenly felt the hairs on the back of my neck prickle.

When I opened my eyes and twisted my head, taking those in around me my head, I felt my breath stall in my chest.

Those eyes.

Those mesmerizing gray eyes of his were on me.

And. They. Were. Heated.

Suddenly, all I wanted to do was to dance erotically, just for him.

Pretend that everyone in the room faded away, and it was just the two of us.

Or I wanted to be the big girl that I was and stalk over to him, climb onto his lap, whisper in his ear to clear the clubhouse out, and ride the heck out of him.

Was it getting hot in here?

Or was it just me?

"What are you waiting for?" I jumped when I heard Stella's voice in my ear.

My head whipped around to look at her, and I asked, "Wha... what are you talking about?"

She smiled that all-knowing smile of hers and then wrapped a hand around the side of my neck, "Chloe, you're my best friend. And if I didn't think that you were perfect for my dad, I'd ditch you so fast your head would spin."

What?

Was she saying what I think she's saying?

At the bewildered look on my face, she snickered, "Go to him. Be with him. All I ask is that you love him. And I already know that you do."

"Stell..." she brought her hand up, halting my words.

She chuckled, then lowered her hand, "I love you, Co. Go to him."

I swallowed.

"How are you not mad at me?" I asked.

Her mouth opened and closed, then she asked, "What on earth for?"

I swallowed, "For not telling you sooner. And all the times you asked when something was bothering me?"

She smiled, "If you were anyone else, Co, I would hate you forever. But you're not. You're my Co. Just know that I come first. You were mine first. Okay?"

I nodded, then reached out and hugged her.

She returned it and then whispered, "You hid it as best you could, but my dad damn sure didn't."

I pulled away and looked at her with wide eyes.

She shook her head and smiled, "Come on, Co. You're one of the smartest people I know. He bites the head off of anyone who interrupts him when he's busy. He even gives me the finger and tells me to wait. But do you know who he doesn't do that to?"

"Me," I whispered.

She nodded, "Yeah. You."

Then I sighed because she was right.

In every instance.

And then, when my feet didn't move fast enough for her liking, she chuckled and then gave me a shove.

When she did that, my eyes were on Asher.

And when I stumbled forward, I watched as his hands clenched into tight fists on his lap.

Oh. My.

Taking in a deep breath for courage, I looked back at Stella, only to see her throw me two thumbs up.

My eyes landed back on Asher, and when I saw crinkles forming at the corners of his eyes, I hid a small smile.

The moment I reached him, I said, "So, Stella thinks I'm perfect for you."

He looked up at me, tilted his head, and nodded, "Because you are."

With those three words, I took in the man that was Asher.

The man who had never once lied to me.

The man that I trusted above all others.

And when I saw something akin to hunger in those hazel eyes of his with flecks of gold in them, I swallowed.

Heat. Passion. Need. Trust. And love.

Then, like a clumsy newborn giraffe, I climbed onto his lap.

My thighs were on the outsides of his, my hands wrapped around the back of his neck.

And then, he looked at me, his face coming closer to mine, and there, against my lips, he whispered, "Took you long enough."

I felt my breath catch.

The moment I had been waiting for. For well over a decade, it was finally about to happen.

However, right before his lips could touch mine, the doors to the clubhouse opened.

And when I looked in that direction, as did everyone else, I noticed two things.

Asher's body stiffened.

And Stella's face went white. Pale white.

Then her eyes came to me, and I couldn't read the look on her face.

But it was gone before I could even try, then her eyes glanced at Asher, and then she looked at the woman.

The woman, dressed in a pair of red wide-legged pants and a fluffy white blouse, said, "Hey, sweet pea," and I saw she was looking at Stella.

Then her gaze moved, and when her eyes landed on me, she looked over slightly and then at Asher, and weirdly, with a small laugh, she said, "Hey, honey, I'm home."

My head whipped around to look at Asher, and I asked, "Who is she?"

Asher didn't respond to me. But I did see that familiar tick in his jaw.

The vein in his throat was throbbing.

But then... he turned his head and stared into my eyes, and I watched as the corners softened ever so slowly.

Then he lifted me up and off his lap ever so carefully sat me back down in the seat. His face was barely an inch away from mine, and he whispered, "Be patient with me. Okay?"

I didn't respond.

I didn't even move.

Because not even a second later, my gaze moved to the woman, and when she moved her hand and revealed a single gold band on a very important finger, my world felt as though it had tilted on its axis.

Asher moved away from me, tagged the woman around the waist, and pulled her to his office.

Stella moved with them.

And then... when I felt a ton of eyes on me, I took them in, and one thing I saw reflected in them... remorse.

Yeah, I definitely didn't have a good feeling about that woman.

Who the hell was she?

Just then, my phone rang, and when I saw it was my boss, I stood up and answered it.

I had been working for Sheridan Accounting Services since I graduated college, and I loved it.

My boss, Brandon Sheridan, wanted to let me know that one of the oldest accounts we had needed to be gone through with a fine-tooth comb. Something wasn't looking right.

So, I told him I would do that first thing Monday morning when I got back into the office.

After I finished the call, I headed back inside the clubhouse, but I froze when I heard what I did.

"Damn, that woman always creates a mess. How the fuck has she been able to hide from him for so long?" Stoney asked.

"Not a damn clue," Priest mumbled out.

"Think she'll sign while she's here?" Whit asked.

"She better. Cause I'll tell you one thing. She doesn't; Asher won't ever get Chloe the way he wants her." I heard Rome mumble.

Sign? Sign what?

Trigger spoke up, then, "Yeah, you know how she is. She's one of the good ones. I don't blame Asher a single bit. But he better hope Chloe is patient if that bitch doesn't sign the divorce paperwork."

At those words, my legs gave out from beneath me.

Chapter 13

Asher

Once the door closed behind Evelyn, I spun and snarled, "What the fuck?"

Her face paled, then she held up her hands, and my eyes caught on that fucking gold band I had slid on her finger almost twenty-one years ago.

Evelyn sighed, then met my eyes and said, "I met someone. And we would like to get married."

I snapped, "Well, that could have happened seventeen years ago if you hadn't turned into a ghost and made it impossible to fucking find you."

She winced, then she looked at Stella.

I wouldn't have made a good mother," she said.

Stella scoffed, "What you mean is that you weren't a decent human being."

"You can say that again," And then, before I could move around my desk to pull open the drawer where the divorce papers were, there was a sudden quick rap succession of knocks on my door.

I glared at Evelyn, pointed my finger at her, and bit out, "Don't move."

Then I moved around her, threw the door open, and growled, "What?"

Stoney growled, "Something's wrong with Chloe, Pres." In a split second, I took in his words, and then I was racing around him and headed for my woman.

And when I found her, I felt as though someone had reached into my chest and pulled my heart out.

She was sitting on her ass, her back against the wall, her legs pulled close to her chest, her slight shoulders shaking.

And I knew. I just knew when I got her eyes, I would see nothing but tears in them.

Only two people were to blame for that.

Evelyn.

And myself.

Because I should have hired the best private investigators to find her and paid no matter how much it would cost to get it all done before I dared to let this beautiful woman anywhere near me.

I knew she felt me coming because her head jerked up, and her eyes hit mine; I almost had to take a step back at the torment that blazed in those sage green eyes of hers I adored.

In the next instant, she was using the wall for support, standing up, rising to her full height.

"Tell me," she demanded as tears trailed down her cheeks.

"Doll Baby, please, don't do this." I pleaded with her.

Hoping beyond hope that she wouldn't walk away from me over this.

But the longer I denied her request to tell her who that woman was, the more I knew.

I knew that she would go.

And then I would lose my reason for breathing.

The reason I got up in the morning.

My very own redemption after a life of pure and utter hell.

"Tell. Me. Who. That. Woman. Is." Gritting out each word through her teeth while those tears flowed down her cheeks almost had me going to my knees.

I thought about lying to her.

Thought about telling her a white lie.

But I knew that she would see through it.

She knew me better than I knew myself.

So, with everything to lose, knowing this would gut her, yet unable to force a lie through my vocal cords, I said the two words that were going to end us before we even had a chance to really begin, "My wife."

That was when I watched the strongest woman I have ever met hit her knees and sob.

Broken, painful sobs poured out of her.

And the sight of it wrenched my heart right out of my chest.

Because I was the dumb motherfucker that had caused it all.

At the sounds she was making, I heard boots thundering through the clubhouse, headed in our direction.

But I never took my eyes off Chloe.

My arms moved of their own accord, my hands skimming her skin, wanting, needing to haul her in my arms, bury my face in her hair, and apologize.

But just as she felt the contact of my hands on her, she flinched.

She. Fucking. Flinched.

That was when I heard Priest rumble, "What the fuck?"

Rome grumbled out, "She okay?"

"Co?" my daughter asked.

At my daughter's voice, Chloe lifted her head.

Tears were streaming down her pale cheeks.

I wanted to pull my gun out and shoot my own fucking self at the sight of those fucking tears.

Chloe looked up at Stella and brokenly asked, "Did you know?"

Stella winced, then carefully, she asked, "Did I know what?"

But before I could get any words out, Chloe did, "That… that your… dad is still… married?"

I watched as my daughter's heart broke right along with Chloe's as her face crumbled right before my eyes, in a broken whisper, she said, "I'm so sorry."

Chloe's breath hitched as she asked, "You knew?"

And all my daughter could do was nod.

As if this situation couldn't get any worse, my bitch of a fucking wife chose the worst moment in time to walk back here with everyone else.

"What's going on in here, Asher? Why is our daughter crying, and why is her best friend looking like she got her heart ripped out?" Evelyn asked.

How did she know about Chloe?

How the fuck did she know that they were best friends?

Someone's head was going to fucking roll.

Flo gasped then, "Shit, was that a secret? I'm so sorry. I met Evelyn a few days ago, and I may have said too much. I'm really sorry."

I would deal with Flo later. She should have known that what occurred in the clubhouse didn't leave it.

My bitch of a wife didn't deserve a response, and thankfully, no one gave her one.

My eyes were trained on Chloe, walking slowly over to her, I knelt in front of her. Silently pleading her with my eyes to give me those sage green eyes that pulled me in and never let me go, to look at me.

"Doll Baby, please, just hear me out. Please."

"Did you make vows to her?" she asked in a broken murmur that had my heart clenching in my chest.

"I did, but baby, please…" I started to say but was rendered speechless when she gave me those eyes I had thought I wanted to see, and then I was gutted when she did.

Pain.

Turmoil.

Hatred.

Fury.

"You owe me a marker, right?" she asked me.

Swallowing down my fear at not knowing what she was going to say, I nodded, "Yes, Doll Baby, I do."

Evelyn asked, "Why the hell do you keep calling her Doll Baby?'

And that was when Creature rumbled out with his scarred-up vocal cords, "Because the sun rises and sets on Chloe in Asher's eyes."

Chloe locked tear-filled eyes with mine and said, "I want you to step back from me, leave me alone, and let me go."

I shook my head, "Please don't ask me to do that. Fucking anything but that."

When she didn't reply, I said, "I'm on my knees right now in front of you, baby, please, please don't ask me to do that."

Brokenly, she whispered, "You're married, Asher.

I wanted to pull her in my arms so badly, but I didn't because I knew my woman, and she was that, she would always be that. "Then let me explain the situation."

Then Evelyn decided to open her mouth and ask, "What situation?"

Standing up, I whirled on her, ready to let loose a string of profanity on her, until I saw that head of gorgeous head of dark hair running around me, around my brothers in the hall.

"Chloe, please," I said as I started to rush after her until my brothers, my fucking brothers blocked my path.

However, it was Whit who spoke, "Give her a breather, brother. You know who Chloe is. We told you before you made your move that you needed to tell her."

Stoney stepped around me, "I got her."

I watched his back until he disappeared out the door.

I locked eyes with Trigger, then I pointed at Flo, "Talk to her before I do. And I let Creature have her."

Chloe

I knew I was in no condition to drive right now.

In the mood I was in, I was either going to get myself killed or someone else.

That was why I veered around the clubhouse and out back, where I knew no one would be.

But what I didn't know was that someone had followed me.

I can't tell you why it hit me like it did. I can't explain it, no matter how hard I tried, I just can't.

But I didn't know that I had said all of that aloud, and neither did I know that someone had been listening to me.

"He's not mine. I don't have a right to be feeling this way." I said as I dropped my head back and took in the night sky.

Not until a voice sounded in the dark, "But don't you?"

Looking over my shoulder, it was to see Stoney, and to his question, I shrugged. And didn't even care that he had been listening to me rambling.

I watched as he made his way over to me, took the chair beside mine, and sat down in it, then he said, "Chloe, you and the Pres. have this bond, a bond that none of us could ever even begin to understand."

I shook my head, "That doesn't matter. He isn't mine."

Stoney winked, "Something doesn't technically have to be yours for you to feel hurt."

My head tilted to the side, and I asked, "How so?"

"Pres. has been yours for the longest time. Honestly, I can't recall a time when he hasn't been yours. And vice versa. We've all seen it. We all know it. It's why we also run interference with other clubs when they come to the clubhouse, and you are there."

I thought back on it.

And realized he was right.

Any time a guy came up to me and tried to talk to me, almost all of the brothers at one point or another have come over and guided that guy away.

I always thought it was because they wanted to talk club business.

I narrowed my eyes at Stoney, "Well played."

He chuckled, and then he sobered. "Your feelings are your own, Chloe. I will say this: if the situation was reversed, Asher would be feeling the same way as you. I'd put every single cent in my name on that fact."

Just then, my phone chimed with a text.

Looking at the screen, I asked myself, why was I agreeing to this?

"That him?" Stoney asked.

I shook my head, looked at Stoney, and mumbled, "No."

Then I looked at Stoney, took in his features, and sighed. I knew he wasn't going to let me get away with simply saying no.

And the longer we sat there, the longer he stared at me.

My mouth was opening and blurting the words out before I could even stop myself, "One of the women I work with has a son. She's been on me about accepting a date from him. And well, I guess you can blame it all on a weak moment... but I said yes."

He stared at me, then tossed his head back and laughed.

I shook my head at him, "It isn't that funny." I mumbled.

He righted his head, looked at me, tapped me on my nose, and said, "Oh, but it is. I can tell you this: I don't think this world has ever seen Asher be a caveman or a Neanderthal, but they are about to."

And with that, he got up and walked away, all the while chuckling as he did so.

I adored Stoney. I truly did.

There was just something about him.

He was that pseudo-grandfather you never knew you needed.

And when you needed him, he was always there.

***

Just like a certain individual, I wished I wasn't around...

It's been thirty-six hours, forty-eight minutes, and thirty-five seconds since the world I knew seemed to exist.

When I saw Pagan sitting on the bench outside my office, I tagged my cellphone, opened the app, and pressed Asher's name because enough was enough.

He answered in a hopeful tone, "Doll Baby."

I snapped, "You lost the right to call me that. You should have told me."

"I know. But fucking hell, Do... Chloe. I couldn't stay away from you. I just couldn't."

"Well, there's nothing we can do about it now. But you better tell Pagan to stop following me everywhere," I growled at him.

If anyone else did this to Asher, I knew they would have been acquainted with the pavement in the blink of an eye.

His raspy tone came over the line, and he said, "I can't do that. Gotta know you're safe and protected, or else I can't sleep at night."

I growled at his words, any other day, any other time before I found out he was married, I would have swooned over.

But today was not that day.

To prove that point, I hit the *End Call* button, put my phone on silent, set it down, and allowed myself a few minutes to deep breath.

Because if I didn't, I would be crying a-freaking-gain.

Jesus, but just how many tears could one person produce?

Apparently, the world wasn't through with playing with Chloe for the week.

Pagan didn't stop following me.

I stubbed my toe when I got home that evening and managed to somehow break the skin when I did so.

Which caused blood to drop on my white carpet.

Oh, and let's not forget to mention that I forgot to get tampons.

Freaking great.

Good thing I had pads.

So, there was that, I figured.

And I meant it by the world wasn't through playing with me.

After I used the bathroom, fixed my toe, and spot-treated the blood spots, there was a knock on the front door.

Since my parents were out for a date night, I knew the visitor could only be here to see me.

I sighed, moved to it, and when I saw it was Stella, I dropped my head against the door and sighed again.

She called out, "I know you're in there, Co. Pagan said so. Please let me in. We've never gone this long without seeing each other since the second grade."

And she... blast it all, was right.

Furthermore, I knew she wouldn't leave until she saw me.

And I was tired.

I wanted to get in my comfortable clothes, grab a pint of ice cream, curl up in my bed, eat my fill, and then pass out.

That was the only reason I unlocked the door, opened it, and moved to the side.

She moved in, smiled at me, with sorrow and regret emanating from her, and then she moved to the couch.

She opened her mouth when she sat down, but I held out my hand for her not to, then moved to sit on the chair opposite the couch.

"We've been friends since second grade, Stell. And not once. Not freaking once did you ever tell me that your dad and your mother were married."

Stella winced, "It was only a formality because she got pregnant with me, Co. I swear to you."

"It doesn't matter. Legally, he's still hers. And when they signed that paper, that also meant vows were exchanged. It didn't matter if they were voiced or not.

Marriage is a big deal." I told her. And she knew how I felt.

Which was why I still don't understand how she could know that, know everything about me, and ever think I would be okay with being with someone who was someone else's.

Stella nodded, "I know that. But in Dad's heart, where it matters, he's yours. He's been yours since our seventeenth birthday."

I narrowed my eyes, "What are you talking about?"

She nodded, "Dad and I talked. And I mean, we had a long talk, Co. Dad told me that he started noticing things about you at our sixteenth birthday party. And by the time you were seventeen, he felt as though someone had reached inside and pulled every organ in his body out. And that happened every single time he fucked someone else because he felt like he was cheating on you. Cheating on his heart."

She kept her gaze locked with mine as she continued, "After the third time it happened, he didn't do it again. He hasn't been with another woman in years Co. Think about it. Dad doesn't lie. Dad doesn't sugarcoat anything. He's blunt. We're twenty-one now, Co."

I shook my head, "While that's nice to hear, it still doesn't negate the fact that he's married."

She shook her head, "So, you're going to miss out on the best thing that's ever happened to you and break my dad's heart."

I got it.

She was loyal to her dad.

I couldn't fault her for that.

But I couldn't fault her for breaking her promise to me.

And I told her as such, "Do you remember when we watched, *Diary of a Mad Black Woman*?"

She looked confused for a moment, and then she nodded. "Yeah, but what does that have to do with anything?"

"I asked you to make me a promise. Do you remember?" I asked as I looked at her.

Her eyes widened, and then I watched as shame colored her features, "Yeah."

And that promise consisted of if I ever let a man step out on me for any reason or make me the other woman, then I wanted her to get me as far away from that man as possible.

I smiled sadly, "I need time to forgive you. I still love you. But I need time."

She shook her head, "But why will you offer that to me and not Dad? That I don't understand."

I felt the tears coming, and I tried to fight them, "Because you only hurt my feelings. What he did... he ripped my heart out and crushed it with his boot."

Stella didn't say anything to that.

No, she knew me.

She knew that once I made my mind up, I was done.

That was why I sat there as I watched Stella walk out of the house.

Only then did I get in my comfortable pajamas, grab the ice cream and a spoon, and curl up in my bed, and yes, I ended up crying myself to sleep.

The only good thing to come from all of this was that I got a raise at work, which allowed me to move out of my parent's house.

All the while I moved, I ignored the men on the bikes who tried to step in and help the movers I had called.

Each one of them, before they gave up trying to help, shared some words with me.

All of them consisted of *Asher was a dumbass. But he tried to end things with her before he pursued you. Give him credit, Chloe.*

In my head, I knew they were right. But my heart... well... it didn't agree.

Three days later, when I went to pay my rent, I smiled at the landlord and gave her my name and apartment number.

She typed it into the computer, read something, and then looked at me, "You're good."

I tilted my head to the side, "Sorry?"

"You're paid up for the next year, Hun. You're good."

"I don't understand. I haven't even paid this month's rent yet. How am I good?"

She lifted a brow, then looked back at her screen, "Says here that a payment was processed for twelve months of rent paid the day after you signed your lease."

And that was when it hit me: that fudge stick of a man.

"Can you tell me who paid it?" I asked through gritted teeth.

When she said his name, I growled, thanked her, and stomped up to my apartment.

... Perhaps this was immature of me, but I didn't care.

I told him to leave me alone and to let me go.

But could that man do that?

Apparently freaking not.

So, that was why I found myself packing up all my belongings, calling a moving company, and out of that apartment in four days.

The new place I moved to was on the other side of town, but I was still smart and thinking. It was still in Zagan MC territory.

See, I wasn't stupid.

Immature maybe.

But not bloody stupid.

I had just walked into my apartment after a long day of being on my feet when my phone rang.

I pulled it out of my bag and checked the caller, and then I narrowed my eyes.

I still hadn't gotten control of my temper and what I wanted to say to him.

So, that was why I silenced the call and then dropped my phone back in my bag.

Kicked my heels off and made myself something for dinner.

Chapter 14

Asher

She fucking moved.

She. Fucking. Moved.

And I fucking needed her.

Fucking hell.

Remember when I said when her temper was riled, I loved the fuck out of it?

I still did.

But this woman was a pain in my ass.

But she was mine.

And she would be mine until the day I took my last breath and the world turned to ash.

However, I had to get her to hear me out. To explain.

Chloe was smart.

She was the smartest woman I knew.

And she would get it.

I had no doubt about that.

If only I could get her to listen to me for five minutes.

I laughed to myself.

Here I was, trying to get my woman back, the only woman I've ever loved, and I was technically still a married man to another woman.

And that woman...

Almost twenty-one years ago.

Fuck, but he loved the open road.

There was nothing like riding a bike down an open road.

Feeling the breeze on your skin.

Nothing out in front of you but asphalt, scenery, and your bike's front tire.

I didn't have any entanglements. Nothing was holding me down.

Nothing was tying me down.

Until I heard about a sex trafficking ring.

And thankfully, I had made friends in my life. Good friends.

Those good friends were all for starting a one-percenter motorcycle club and putting a stop to it.

However, what I never planned for, and didn't want, was for the woman I had fucked months ago to come find me and tell me she was pregnant.

Now, I was raised to be a good man by my parents before they were killed in a car accident by a drunk piece of shit.

That was my first kill.

How the fuck he got off with killing two people while being intoxicated with a slap on the wrist, I didn't know. But I set out to make it right.

So being the good man I was raised to be, I married her, and in name only, so I could put her on my insurance, it was a bitch, but it was better than nothing.

Even though I loved the open road, I came to learn that I loved my club and my daughter more.

Because the day she was placed in my arms, everything felt right.

The location I was in. Everything.

She was the apple of my eye.

Even though the marriage was on paper only, I tried to make it work for my daughter's sake.

However, that stopped working when I got home from a run, heard my four-year-old daughter crying in her room, and heard sounds coming from my bedroom.

Sounds that shouldn't be coming from there.

At fucking all.

Not unless I was in that bedroom.

Therefore, after I made sure my daughter was okay, I tucked her back into bed, turned her little music box on, closed the door, and stalked to my bedroom.

They were still going at it.

Nothing would have surprised me at this point. Absolutely nothing.

Which was why, for the life of me, it didn't bother me seeing my own flesh and blood, my uncle not by blood, pounding into my wife.

I stood there, and when he hit a particular spot in her overused cunt, I started clapping.

But I stopped clapping when that mother fucker looked over his shoulder, smiled at me, and said, "Now that I've fucked your wife. When your daughter is old enough, I'll be railing inside of her. It's the least that you owe me. Their money should have been mine."

I didn't recall pulling my piece out.

I didn't recall putting the silencer on.

I only recalled not wanting to wake my daughter.

I didn't recall the way his brains splattered all over the wall.

I didn't recall my bitch of a wife screaming.

No, the only thing I recalled was telling her to get the fuck out of my sight and to stay gone.

My brothers showed up: Stoney, Priest, Ox, Whit, and Trigger.

They helped me clean the bedroom and got rid of the evidence and her shit.

And that night, I slept like a fucking baby.

Everything was going to shit.

See, when Priest had come to me a few months ago, it was to tell me that he found some shit out about his wife, Trudy.

I would get to that when I spoke to Chloe.

Because if I thought about it now, I was liable to find a woman who didn't mind beating the shit out of another woman and letting her go to town on that bitch.

Now, I needed Chloe.

I needed to talk to her.

I needed to get some of this shit off my chest.

I only hoped like fuck she still felt that she wanted to be my quiet place in a crazy storm.

And it was also time for me to explain everything else to her.

The love of my life, the other part of my soul. And hope like fuck she forgave me.

But I wasn't so sure she would.

I knew about her beliefs.

It turned her stomach for a person not to be faithful to their partner.

It was stupid, immoral, and downright nasty, her words.

And fuck of it all, she was right. One hundred percent right.

That was why when Pagan told me she was home after a day of her running her ass off at work, I called her.

As soon as her voicemail came on, "Hi, you've reached Chloe. I'm not available right now. Leave me a message," I spoke the moment the beep sounded.

"Doll Baby, need you to call me back. It's fucking important. I know you're pissed at me, but I fucking need you."

I hung up and then stared at my phone.

Stared at the picture on my lock screen.

I had said something that had caused Chloe to close her eyes and smile, and my lips were pressed to her forehead.

Damn, but I loved this photo.

My daughter had taken it, just at the right moment, and sent it to me.

I dropped my head back and sighed.

Just then, my daughter came walking over, and she had told me what Chloe said to her.

Honestly, I was at a loss on what to do.

And I knew she felt torn, but she was still her daddy's little girl, and she proved that when she asked, "Dad, what can I do?"

I looked over at my daughter and shrugged because I didn't know what she could do.

What could any of us do?

This whole situation was so beyond fucking up that I couldn't even wrap my head around it.

Two hours later, I was pulling Priest off Trigger and out of the ring we had out back when my phone rang.

When I heard the ringtone, I released Priest and didn't even pay attention to whether he went back into the ring or not because I was walking away while pulling out my phone and hitting that answer button in the next second.

I answered the call and breathed out, "Chloe."

She sighed, then she said, "What is it?"

I didn't smile, even though I wanted to, that fucking temper of hers, "I need you to come to the clubhouse. Please?"

She sighed, "Asher..."

I ran my hand through my hair and then put every ounce of remorse in my tone and said, "Chloe. Please?"

She sighed again, and then she said, "Okay."

She hung up before I could tell her to be careful.

Something we always said to one another.

And if I hadn't known that I was going to have a long way to go at getting her to forgive me, that alone would have told me as much.

But I sat there, the shot glass of whiskey still in front of me, fifteen minutes later, when the door opened.

I looked at it and felt everything in my word suddenly still.

She was the most gorgeous creature to ever grace this world.

Chloe scanned the main room, and when her eyes locked on me, she slowly made her way over to me.

My eyes trailed her as she did so.

And the moment she got close enough to me to read whatever she saw in my eyes, she stopped next to my chair and then offered me her hand.

And like the dutiful puppy, I was where she was concerned, I stood up, placed my hand in hers, and allowed her to lead me wherever she wanted to take me.

She led me out of the clubhouse, through the back courtyard, and to the gondola I had built so the girls could be outside when it rained.

Knowing what she wanted, I smiled inwardly.

I sat down on the swing and then waited. I didn't have to wait long as she settled on the other end.

That was too far away from me for my liking, but I didn't say anything.

No, all I did was inhale.

Vanilla and strawberries.

It was long moments before she asked, "What's going on?"

I swallowed, then head hanging low, I said, "Remember when Priest came to me after I had painted your toes on your eighteenth birthday?"

I looked up at her then and watched as she stilled, then hesitantly, she asked, "Yeah?"

I nodded, "Well, it was because Priest found evidence of her cheating on him."

Her body locked.

But I continued. "They worked it out. He loved her. But recently, he started seeing the same signs. So, he followed her. Found out she was selling her body for blow."

"What the heck?" Chloe murmured.

"She was the one who asked for a divorce when he made a so-called scene. And that was by grabbing up all the blow he found and flushed it down the toilet."

"Right on, Priest," she whispered.

"Yeah. However, he received something in the mail this morning. From a clinic."

When Chloe didn't respond, I continued, "They are under new management. And somehow, that bill slipped through the cracks."

Hesitantly, she asked, "What was it for?"

"One bill was for a DNA test. And the other was for an abortion," I said.

And I waited.

I didn't have to wait long.

Her body jerked so fast that it was a miracle the swing didn't move too much. Then her eyes swung to mine, and she gasped, "Are you telling me what I think you're telling me?"

"If you think I'm telling you that once she found out it was Priest's baby, she aborted it? You would be thinking the same thing I'm telling you."

"Ese no es un buen pedazo de basura humana." She snapped.

I lifted a brow, "Say that in English for me, yeah?"

"I called her a no good piece of human trash," she snapped.

Her temper was in full force.

I wanted to have the right to pull her into my chest and kiss the hell out of her. This fucking woman.

And she proved her point when she growled, "I want to find her and beat the snot out of her."

"I'll have bail money ready," I said with a wink.

Just then, I opened my mouth to explain the next part of why I wanted to talk to her, however, before I could, Priest stomped out of the clubhouse, a bottle of tequila in his hand.

"Oh shit," I muttered.

Chloe looked at Priest, nodded, and said, "Go to him. Keep him safe. Okay?"

And before I could tell her not to go, that I was thinking the hell with all the bullshit because she was the only one who mattered, she got up and walked away.

Fuck. Me.

Chapter 15

Chloe

My heart broke for Priest.

I was seriously pacing my apartment trying to figure out a way to unalive that woman. She didn't deserve to live.

Who the freaking flip did she think she was?

The nerve of some people.

Just as I moved to make another pass around my living room, there was a knock on my door.

When I moved to it, you could have knocked me over with a feather.

Because standing on the other side of my door was Asher's wife.

I may have seen her in a brief moment, however, for as long as I live, I will never forget her face.

I sighed and decided to be the bigger person; therefore, I opened the door.

And the moment I did, she looked at me, smiled, and asked, "Hi, may I come in?"

I didn't move, no, I said I would be the bigger person, which was why I opened the door, now... everything else was up in the air, I asked, "What are you doing here?"

She smiled sadly, "I came here to maybe help clear things up. I promise not to upset you. And if I do, I'll gladly sit here until Asher arrives and carts me off to places unknown, never to be heard from or seen again."

I lifted a brow, "Why would you do that?"

She smiled, "Because I finally found what I had been looking for all these years. And if I can help you, forgive Asher. Then I'm going to do that. And I hurt my daughter a long time ago. This won't fix everything, and I know that, but maybe it's a start."

I sighed, then opened the door for her.

She smiled and then nodded her thanks.

I was being the bigger person, which was why I offered her a glass of water.

I got myself a beer, and I could have laughed that she sat down on my couch in the same manner that Stella had at my parent's house.

Once she took a sip and cradled the glass, she said, "I know people think that I'm a bad person. And a lot of them would be correct. I was young. Sure, people like you, who have their whole life planned out, would see it that way."

She swallowed and continued, "I wasn't ready to be a mother. I didn't fully understand the concept of loving one person. My parents had what is called an open relationship, and it worked for them. And for a time, it worked for me. Until I slept with Asher's uncle."

I gasped, "Wait, he has an uncle?"

She nodded, "Yeah, he did. You'll have to ask Asher about that. It's not my story to tell. But all I can say is that I was young and stupid. Thought it was cool that this older man who said he had money only wanted to be with me. That was a laugh unto itself. I'll let Asher tell you the full story."

I sighed, another person wanting me to listen to Asher.

"After I left them, I went to Mexico. Had a procedure done. I wasn't motherly. At all. And I knew that I wouldn't change my mind. And all these years later, I still haven't changed my mind. Some women are born to be mothers, and some are definitely not."

"I understand that." was all I said.

"We were young, Chloe. So young. Looking back on it, we never should have gotten married. Asher was never in the wrong about anything he ever did. But I didn't love him. And he sure didn't love me. I mean, I might have thought at one time that we had. I'm not going to lie. But the way he watched you walk away from him? It looked like he was thrown into the fiery gates of hell, had his skin flayed off, and his bones ripped from his body. He was torn and shattered. When I left, he didn't even react. He simply turned and walked back into the house after he watched me flee the house that night."

Then she smiled, sat her glass of water down on the coffee table, opened her phone, and pulled out her phone.

"This is what he looked like when you left. Watch it. Then make up your mind, honey. Because if my man looked like that, and I truly loved him, it would tear me apart."

I looked at her phone, hesitant to take it when she offered it to me, which was why I asked, "Where did you get this?"

She smiled, "Charlie, I told him I was going to talk to you. He got that off a camera in the clubhouse."

Only then did I take the phone from her, sat my beer down, and hit play.

I watched the video again and again and again.

But what caused my emotions to feel as though they had been ignited were the words that rumbled out of him, "Whit, your acting Pres. Until I win her back."

"No. Fuck no." Whit disagreed.

"I'm not the man y'all need without her by my side. I'm better with her there. I'm stronger. And I'm whole. I'm half a man right now."

"You'll get her back," I heard Creature's low tone rumble out.

Rome nodded, "Yeah, she loves you. Everyone knows it. Love like that doesn't simply go away."

After I watched the video one more time, I handed her phone back to her.

"Any man who's willing to walk away from one of the only things he's ever really known for a woman, that says it all right there. Take your time. Think. And thank you for allowing me to talk to you."

And with that, she smiled, got up, and walked out of my apartment.

Sadly, she was right. I had a lot to think about.

I sighed as I looked at the clock, well, I wouldn't be thinking about that tonight.

I had somewhere to be.

Asher

"Umm, pres.... you're not going to like this," Pagan said when I answered the phone.

I growled, "Spit it the fuck out, boy."

"Chloe is on a date." Those four words were like a knife in my belly.

At his words, I stood up so fast that the chair I had been sitting in slammed against the wall.

I only had one thought in mind: grab what I needed and go find my wayward woman.

I stalked to my office and grabbed the divorce decree. Fuck doing this tomorrow. Fuck my plans.

It was happening now, right this very fucking second.

Walking back into the main part of the clubhouse, I barked at Pagan, "Where?"

Once he relayed where that fool woman was, I stalked to the doors, then kicked them open and stormed to my bike.

Arriving at the restaurant, I tore off my helmet, lifted my leg, and planted my other boot on the pavement.

Reaching into my saddlebags, I tagged the gift box I had and then stalked into the restaurant.

My eyes immediately scanned the inhabitants.

Some woman standing at the hostess stand said, "Sir, can you tell me the name of the party you are looking for?"

I, of course, ignored her.

Looking left, then right, my eyes hit every single female in this building, and then when my eyes landed on my heart that was sitting in a booth across from some punk ass motherfucker I growled and then stalked over to their booth.

The moment I reached her table, I ignored the limp dick-looking mother fucker and slammed my divorce decree down on the table in front of her.

Then I laid the box down in front of her, and then I walked the fuck out, sat down on my bike, and waited.

And then I waited, then waited, and then waited some more.

When I didn't see her, I got up off my bike and stormed back into the restaurant.

The hostess didn't bother saying a word to me.

When I reached her table, I said, "Gave you time to walk your gorgeous ass out to me, Chloe, ain't waiting for another second longer for you to be in my arms."

She sighed, then looked up at me and said, "I'm busy, Asher. And this decree doesn't change anything. You were married. You should have told me. You didn't do that. That's on you."

I braced my hands on her table, lowered my head, locked my eyes with hers, and said, "Well, you're right about one thing. I may have been married to that bitch on paper, but in my heart, I'm married to you. And you can bet your ass, no matter what I have to do, you will be married to me before the sun sets tomorrow."

Her eyes flared, and I watched as they softened slightly, I would take that.

I would even take her temper she was about to throw at me, which she did in the next instance.

She threw her hands up and snapped, "You think I'm going anywhere with you? You've lost your ever-loving mind.

I grinned, "Chloe, I divorced her ass. I'm fucking yours."

She snapped, her voice raising, and I didn't give two shits if we gave the customers a show, "You were hers when you almost kissed me. You made me the other woman. And that's so far from okay that it isn't even funny."

Then I growled to hide my grin, "I never fucking loved her, Chloe. I fucking love you."

I ran my hand through my hair, I didn't plan to tell her like that, "God damnit, Chloe. Just let me explain. Okay. Half an hour, that's all I'm asking you for. You fucking owe me that much."

And that was the wrong thing to say, and I knew it when she gasped, stood, grabbed the glass of water in front of her, and then threw its contents in my face.

Then she looked at the limp-dick motherfucker I was having a hard time with, not slamming his face into the table for even daring to spend even two minutes in her breathable atmosphere.

"I'm so sorry, Mr. Everett. I apologize on behalf of Sheridan Accounting for our meeting being ruined. Please accept my deepest apologies and take in everything about our company before this rude individual interrupted our meeting when you make your decision. Thank you, and I hope you have a great weekend."

And with that, she moved me out of her way and stormed out the door.

I stood there as I took in exactly what I just did. Then I ran my hand through my hair and said, "Well, shit."

The man laughed, "I don't envy you. Tell me, would you do it all over again if it meant you got even a minute of her time?"

I looked at him and did one thing: I nodded.

He smiled, "Well, at least you didn't claim to love your wife and then ended up knocking four different women up."

I scoffed, "Damn, man. Nah, I even get around another woman who isn't Chloe, feels like my dick tucks itself into a deep corner and hides."

He laughed.

I sighed and asked, "Anything I could get you to do to go with Chloe and her firm?"

He shook his head, "My mind was already made up before this meeting. This was only a formality. They just didn't know it."

I nodded.

Then I stood up, grabbed my wallet, and tossed some cash that should cover her meal, then looked at the man and said, "No one pays for my woman but me."

He crossed his arms over his chest and nodded.

Then I tagged the divorce decree and the medium sized black box.

Once I got on my bike, I thought about where I needed to go. Where would Chloe go?

But after an hour of looking everywhere for her, I headed to my house.

Only to stop my bike beside her little Honda.

I grinned, I should have known.

And there she was, sitting on one of the rocking chairs, curled up under a red blanket she keeps in her car.

Walking up the steps, she said, "I want to know everything."

I looked into those eyes of hers I wanted to stay lost in.

Then I leaned back on the railing, crossed my arms over my chest, and told her everything.

"So, why did you stay married to her all this time?"

I sighed, then ran my hand through my hair, "She was a vindictive bitch. Told me that if I ever tried to divorce her, she would take the evidence she had of what I did to the feds. Believed her. So, I stayed the course. Allowed her to basically keep hold of my balls technically. Until you were sixteen."

She tilted her head, "Why when I was sixteen?"

"Cause I realized you were the one I had been waiting on all my life. Realized that if I didn't see you, then the sun didn't rise for me. Lived in darkness 'til I saw your eyes."

"Evelyn might have held my balls, but I didn't want her to. I wanted you to be the one. 'Cause if you told me to go jump off a bridge to make you happy, I'd do it. Just to see your smile one more time."

I watched as a tear trailed from the corner of her eye.

I had to beat back the need to move in and wipe it from her cheek.

She sat there, using one foot to rock back and forth, and then she stopped and asked, "You killed your so-called uncle because he slept with your wife?"

He shook his head, "No, I killed my so-called uncle because he thought that if he slept with Evelyn, that meant he could also sleep with Stella when she was old enough."

Vehemently, she gasped then furiously; she shook her head, "Well then, he deserved everything he got."

"I haven't seen her since that day. I should have done more. Should have just pushed everything, but honestly,

I haven't been looking for her as I could have. Didn't really start looking for her until you were eighteen. I'm fucking sorry."

She looked up at me, then nodded. "Okay."

I grinned back, "Okay."

Chapter 16

Chloe

I got it all. I truly did.

And I forgave Asher. Technically, he didn't do anything wrong, even though, at the time, it felt like he had.

I'd talked to Stella, too. Like always, she and I were good.

That was why I opened the box he had left with me, removed the tissue paper, and saw the black leather kutte nestled inside of it.

I smiled as I saw Property of Asher on the back of it.

Bringing it to my nose, I smiled.

Leather and Asher. All rolled into one. There was nothing better.

I'd made my decision.

And it was time to tell him.

As I strode into the clubhouse in black fitted jeans, black heels, a red top, and my property kutte on my back, I smiled at the girls.

Stella came to me first and smiled, "Damn, but that looks good on you."

I smiled at her, "It feels pretty good, too."

"They're in church, don't think dad will mind," and with that, she winked at me, then walked across the floor and knocked on the doors to church.

I stood there waiting with bated breath.

The door opened, and then I saw Trigger's face, he listened to her, then looked over her head.

His eyes widened, and then he smiled.

Then he turned his head and said something.

The next thing I knew, I heard something slam into the wall, then the door was opened wider, and there he stood.

All six-foot-two of glorious muscle, looking hot as sin.

He looked at me, did a top to toe, then he started forward.

I didn't move.

I could feel all the brother's eyes on me as they emptied out of church.

But it was Asher's I was most concerned about.

He stopped just a breath of me and said, "You forgive me?"

I stared into his eyes and asked, "Do you forgive me?"

He lifted a brow, "For what?"

"For being a brat," I said.

He chuckled, "You weren't being a brat, Chloe. Don't think you even know how to be one. What you were was hurt. And that was on me."

I smiled, "Good. So, since I put this thing on, I'm telling the world I'm yours. What are you going to do to prove to the world that you're mine?"

And that was when he shocked me. He winked, took off his kutte, then lifted his t-shirt.

And right there, along his ribs, was my name in beautiful script, which looked familiar.

He laughed, "Found an old letter you wrote to Stella. She was okay with me taking it to my tattoo guy."

"Only one thing we need to do," he said as he lowered his shirt and stepped closer to me.

I smiled, "Yeah, what's that?"

His hand still holding his kutte wrapped around my waist, his other hand wrapped around my neck, and then I lost all train of thought as his head lowered, I rose on my tiptoes, and against my lips, he whispered, "This."

Then he kissed me.

And oh my, if I ever thought that a kiss was supposed to be simple... then I needed to have my brain looked at.

Because this kiss was anything but simple.

It was soul-shattering.

Earth quaking.

The kind of kiss you would bleed for.

The kind of kiss you would die for.

His tongue teased my lips, and my hands clenched in his shirt, he put pressure on my neck; it moved, and then I allowed his tongue to enter my mouth.

The delicate way his tongue teased mine... I always thought it was weird when authors wrote about spontaneously coming with just a kiss. But I had officially felt it. Oh. My.

When we pulled away, he rested his forehead on mine, then he whispered, "Fucking love you, Chloe."

I smiled, then whispered, "I love you more."

Our moment was interrupted by Stella.

"Just saying, but I will not be calling you Mom," Stella said with merriment dancing in her light gray eyes.

I giggled, "Good. Because that would be freaking weird."

Asher looked at me and winked, "Now she's a brat."

I threw my head back and laughed, and all the while, Asher watched with a smile on his handsome face.

A little while later, I was sitting in his lap; his hands were running through my hair, and then I did something I'd been wanting to do for years.

I snuggled up into Asher, resting my head on his shoulder and burying my face in his neck.

Taking in a deep breath, the scent that was all Asher filled my senses.

Pressing a kiss to his throat, I closed my eyes.

Then I asked, "Think you can ask everyone to leave for a little while?"

He didn't hesitate, "Trigger?"

How Trigger heard him over the music, I didn't know, but I was grateful for it.

His eyes never once left mine, he said, "Get the fuck out."

Trigger chuckled, then once everyone was out of the clubhouse, the moment, the very moment the last person left and the door closed, it happened.

His lips met mine, and then I lost all train of thought.

His lips felt so soft against my own.

I didn't think about if I was doing this right.

I didn't think about anything other than the feel of him.

His hands moved to the tops of my thighs, rubbing slowly while his tongue teased at my lips.

The moment I opened my mouth and gave him entry into a place no other has ever been, I couldn't tell you where he began and I ended.

It was just that magnificent.

He pulled his lips away from mine, his hands skimming up and down my thighs, and then he whispered, "Fucking finally."

I grinned, then leaned in and kissed him.

And that kiss... well... I can tell you that if we had been an official couple, I would have broken the *Guinness Book of World Records* for how fast I took my clothes off.

His lips pulled from mine, and then he whispered, "Just so we're on the same fucking page here. We're taking this at your pace."

I grinned, "As long as you're mine, I don't care about anything else."

He winked, "Been yours since you were seventeen, Doll Baby. You just never noticed."

Suddenly, there was a knock on the front door.

Asher's eyes glinted, then he called out, "Yeah?"

"Is it safe to come back in?" Trigger asked.

I giggled.

But Asher just watched me.

I lifted a brow at him, "What?"

He chuckled, "Waiting on you to tell me what you want to do. This is your world. I'm just living in it."

For the umpteenth time that night, I forgot how to breathe.

And when he saw that, he chuckled, then dragged his right hand up my side, the column of my neck to settle in my hair.

He tugged it gently, then said, "We can let them back in. Or we can tell them to fuck off. Doesn't make a fucking difference to me. As long as you don't leave your spot on my lap."

I lifted a brow again, then asked, "And what if I have to pee?"

He shrugged. "Then I'll be carrying you to the bathroom, letting you do your business, then your back in my arms where you fucking belong."

I grinned, then muttered, "Caveman."

He winked, "Only like that with you."

I grinned, "Let them back in."

He winked, "Yes, ma'am."

Once he gave the order, everyone filed in, and all their eyes were on the two of us.

Priest marched over and asked, "So, are you two finally together?"

I smiled down at Asher. He lifted a brow, and I knew he was waiting for my answer.

I grinned, "Yeah. He's mine."

Priest whistled, then said, "It's about fucking time."

"Shots. We gotta celebrate this shit. Our Pres. finally found a woman worthy of his cantankerous ass." Trigger boomed.

Pagan was behind the bar pouring shots.

Stoney brought two over to Asher and me.

With the shot glass in his hand, he winked at me, "Here's to me breaking my back to make sure you never regret your decision here tonight."

I smiled, then lifted my shot glass to his, "And here's to me being your quiet place in a crazy storm."

I watched as he took in my words, swallowing as he did so, and then he was crushing his lips to mine.

I drank in his kiss.

I reveled as his tongue swept along to mine.

We were both breathless when we separated.

With our clink of glasses, we both downed our shot.

Minutes later, his hand was still running through my hair while his other hand was rubbing up and down my back.

And just like that, I fell asleep.

What I didn't know was that once Asher surmised I had done this, he had called out to have the music lowered.

***

Since Asher had become mine and I had become his, I was smiling from ear to ear these days.

It's been three weeks.

Three weeks of kisses and stolen touches.

And as the days passed, I was getting even closer to closing that final gap between us.

And giving him all of me.

Because you can bet your sweet behind that, I wanted all of him.

It was only fair, after all.

***

After he had church two days ago, I was informed that when he got back from his run, he was taking me out on a proper date. And I couldn't wait.

Stella and I had even gone out and bought me a new dress.

I wasn't lying as I said I had been smiling from ear to ear these days.

And I was getting asked about it at work.

When I told them that Asher and I had finally gotten together, two of the women had been happy for me, one of them had huffed and mumbled about being closer to age to him than I was. But I snickered.

And told her that age was just a number.

And it was.

That fact was further proved as I recalled what he told me over the phone just last night.

He was on a run with Rome, Coal, and Priest.

"Whenever you're ready to give me all of you, all you gotta do is tell me. We are taking this at your pace. Long as I have you, I don't give a damn."

And I knew that he meant it.

Because Asher Samuel Hendrix didn't say anything he didn't mean.

We had been out back by the fire pit, and I had a few things I wanted to know about him.

One of them was his full name. He already knew mine because Stella thought it was funny.

I was named Chloe Britt Whitman. And seeing as CBW stood for Chemical and biological warfare. She told me I needed to come with a warning label.

Unlike her name, Stella Bell Hendrix, which was cool.

And I wanted to know about his parents, his life, and I wanted to know basically everything.

And under a sheet of stars, we talked well into the pre-dawn hours.

But I missed something I treasured.

When I fell asleep, he had carried me into the clubhouse, up the stairs, and up to his bed.

And I couldn't even begin to explain the feeling when I woke up the next morning to his lips on my forehead as he whispered, "Good Morning, Doll Baby."

***

But now was now.

I was in my bedroom, curling my hair while my parents were making dinner in my kitchen. Since their stove had gone out this morning, I had offered up the use of my kitchen.

I had just finished curling my hair when my mama called out, "Your young man is here."

I snickered, young man. He was closer to my parent's age than mine. But after the whole Marco ordeal, my parents had accepted our relationship without saying a word.

Have I ever mentioned that my parents were cool?

Because they were that. Indeed cool.

I smiled at my reflection as I turned off the curling iron in my bathroom.

Then, I moved to the floor-length mirror that hung on the back of my bedroom door and took the finished product in.

Dang.

But there was just something about this particular color.

Smiling, I grabbed my clutch, opened my door, and in my three-inch patent leather pumps, I headed down the hall.

Asher was standing with his back to me, talking to my father.

And when he obviously heard me coming, he looked over his shoulder, stopped mid-conversation, and stared.

I had one thought on my mind, well, two really, one was that he looked incredible.

And two, I wanted him to look at me just like that when I walked down the aisle to him.

Because one day, I was totally marrying this man.

He walked to me as I stopped at the end of the hallway, and then he said, "You're trying to send me to an early grave."

I snickered, "Do you like it?" I asked as I held my arms out at my sides.

He nodded, then rubbed his bottom lip with his thumb, then he said, "Yeah. Fucking love it. But what I had planned for tonight just isn't going to fucking do."

I tilted my head to the side, "And why is that?"

"Doll Baby, you've met me. Right? You know how I am. You've seen how I react when someone looks at you too long. And seeing as this is our first official date as me your man, and you my woman... god damned, Doll Baby. Fucking love you in that dress."

My mother huffed at his language.

He blushed.

He actually blushed.

Then he held his hand out to me to help me down the last step, and once he had my hand in the crook of his arm, he looked at my mama and asked, "What can I do to redeem myself?"

My mama lifted a brow, "You've redeemed yourself for life where I am concerned, but be mindful. Yes?"

He nodded.

Then he shook his hand with my father, and only then did he lead me out the door and to his truck.

And I knew he got a kick out of helping me into it.

That was by placing his hand on my ass.

And he was right, he told me about his plans, and I knew that wouldn't be good.

Even though the restaurant had great food, it wasn't worth all the pretentious men who no doubt would be there and didn't think anything about looking at other women when they were out with a woman.

However, he looked at me and winked, "Don't think I won't show you off, Doll Baby."

And he did that in more ways than one.

He just had all the brothers at the marina form a barricade around us so no one could get a good look at me and to keep me safe.

For two hours, we wandered along the marina, eating and laughing, and it was as if the brothers weren't even there.

Not even when we made it to one section, Asher at my back, my front pressed to the railing, fireworks going off in the night sky, my head turned to the side, his lips on mine.

It was perfect.

Absolutely perfect.

However, what wasn't perfect was three days later, and Asher was acting like a petulant toddler.

I thought with age came wisdom.

Apparently, not with my man.

Stubborn... gah...

"This is stupid," Asher mumbled as he carried in another box.

Apparently, Asher didn't like the look of my neighbor in my new apartment after he had brought me home after our date.

So, he had contacted the previous apartment complex and paid I didn't know how much money to get me back into that apartment.

Even though he did all of that without me saying a word to him, he was now acting like a toddler.

I lifted a brow and put my hand on my hip, "Exactly how is this stupid?"

He dropped the box on the stack of boxes in my bedroom, looked at me, and lifted his own brow, "How is this not, Doll Baby? I have a perfectly good house. If you wanna tear it down and build a new one, that's okay with me. If you want to demolish a room, I don't have a problem with it. But you're mine, and I'm yours. So, this whole thing is stupid."

"Asher, you're being ridiculous," I said as I passed by him, but I didn't make it far.

Because the moment I cleared his big frame, he had his hand on my bicep and his other hand on my hip, and he spun me, then backed me into a wall.

Then he lowered his head and got in my face, "I'm not being ridiculous. I want you with me. Always. Spent too much time apart as it is. This is more time apart."

I sighed, then placed my hands on his chest, "Asher, seriously. I get that. And I want to be with you all the time, too. But I need to do this. I don't want to take advantage of you," when he opened his mouth to no doubt say otherwise, I placed my finger over his lips, which he kissed, dork, then I said, "We are starting something new. Yes, I've known you for almost all my life. But I knew you as Stella's dad. The president of Zagan MC. I haven't known you as my man. And vice versa. I signed the contract for a year. I need that, Asher. Please. Plus, you were the one who didn't like my neighbor and did all of that without talking to me about what you wanted to do. That's on you, big guy."

He sighed, then placed his forehead atop mine, "How the fuck do you do that?"

I grinned, "How in the eff do I do what?"

He chuckled, "Get me to stay calm and to see reason. Wait, allow me to rephrase that, to see your reasoning."

I winked up at him, "It's a gift."

He pressed a kiss on my forehead, "You ever going to curse?"

"You have met my mama, right?"

"So, what you're saying is, even though I'm the president of a one percent motorcycle club, and we have kids, I'm going to have to watch my mouth?"

A feeling swept over me.

So soft.

So sweet.

My entire frame warmed. Then I whispered, "When we have kids?"

He nodded, "Yeah. Kids. But we're having boys. 'Cause if we have girls, I really will be in an orange jumpsuit if they look anything like their mama."

"Umm, guys, can you quit with the lovey-dovey stuff? We've got more stuff to do. And Dad, she was mine first. I get to spend the first night with her here. Not you." Stella grinned cheekily.

Asher lowered his voice and whispered, "If she wasn't my daughter..."

I giggled, then shoved him back, moved away from him, looked over my shoulder, and tossed him a wink.

Because my man had totally been checking out my ass in my new pair of cut-off white denim shorts.

After we got everything moved, Stella went to get boxed wine and pizza, Asher and I broke in my new couch because he declared my old one wasn't big enough by hitting first base.

I was getting so close to telling him I was finally ready.

***

It was three days later when my phone at my desk rang, picking it up, I said, "Hello."

Then I smiled when I heard his voice, "Hey, Doll Baby, you weren't answering your phone. You good?"

"Yeah, I'm okay. We just have a lot of work to do today," I told him as I moved on to another client's file.

"Alright. How much longer are you working?"

I sighed, then looked at the clock. "I've got at least three more hours."

"Alright. Head to my place when you get off work." He was smoking a cigar.

God, I knew it was a nasty habit, but I loved the smell of his cigars when he smoked them.

Moreover, I loved laying my head on his chest and smelling that particular scent.

I smiled at the memory from a few days ago.

Then I said, "Sounds good. On one condition."

I heard his smile in his voice, "Yeah, what's that?"

I smiled, "I get a freaking hug."

He chuckled, man, but I lived for making this man chuckle.

Smile.

Laugh.

See that sparkle in his eyes.

He caused me to feel all warm and toasty when he responded with, "Doll Baby, you can have all the hugs."

"Text or call me when you leave, alright?" I smiled.

This man. He wasn't controlling when he asked, and he was being protective.

I smiled like I was doing all the time where he was concerned, and then I said, "10-4, Big Daddy."

He laughed.

However, three hours and forty-five minutes later, I was headed out to my car. The moment I got in, started it, and blasted the heat, I tagged my phone and texted Asher.

Me – *On the way now.*

Asher – *Okay, Doll Baby. Be careful.*

Twenty minutes later, I pulled into Asher's driveway.

The moment I entered his house, he was standing there,

Then he moved, and he moved to wrap me in his arms, and I got my hug.

I pressed a kiss to his chest, right over his heart.

Then he lowered his head and whispered, "This is payback for what you called me earlier.

I scrunched my brows, "Payback for..."

And that was all I got out.

Because one minute I had my head on his chest, and the next I was up and over his shoulder, then being tossed on the couch, and he was tickling me.

"I give up," I said through tears. "I give. I give. Uncle. Uncle."

Asher grinned down at me, and stopped tickling me, then he whispered, "Not your fucking uncle."

I winked up at him, "No. You're my Asher."

He nodded, "Nothing else I'd rather be."

Then we heard Stella's voice, "Okay, I have my eyes closed. If I run face-first into something, I'm sending you the hospital bill."

I giggled, "We're not naked, Stella. Geez."

Her hand lowered slowly, and then her fingers moved so she could peak between them.

I laughed at her.

Stella shook her head, winked at me, then headed to the clubhouse.

Apparently, Asher had cooked us dinner and kept it warm for when I got off work.

His only words were, "You've been working hard. The last thing you need is to cook, Doll Baby."

I rewarded him with a hot, scorching kiss.

And since today was Friday, after we ate a delicious meal that consisted of garlic buttery steak and loaded mashed potatoes, he asked if I wanted to go to the clubhouse.

Since I hadn't seen him as much as I would have liked this past week, I readily agreed.

***

Rock music was flowing out of the speakers.

Good times and good vibes.

Moonshine was in a few cups; shots of whiskey were being thrown back.

And ever since Asher had looked at me with heat in his eyes, I knew.

Thankfully, I'd stuck to soda this entire time.

Which was why I walked over to where he sat in the corner, leaned down, his beard tickled my neck, and there against his ear, I whispered, "Take me home and make me yours in every way possible."

I pulled my head back and took in his eyes, he stared into mine and then asked, "You have anything to drink?"

I grinned, "No."

He winked, stood, and then tossed me over his shoulder.

Catcalls and hoots sounded as he carried me out of the clubhouse and out to his bike.

He sat me on his feet, then wrapped his hand around the side of my neck, "Need to do something first."

I lifted a brow, "And that is?"

He winked, then reached into his kutte, pulled something out, and then did the very last thing I expected.

He dropped to one knee. Right there in the middle of the parking lot outside of the clubhouse.

My hands came to my mouth, and tears formed in my eyes.

Then, like a shield had been moved from his eyes, those amazing hazel eyes with tawny flecks in them showed me every emotion a woman wants to see in the man she loves.

Want. Need. Heat. Hunger. Love.

"You were seven years old the first time I met you. And I didn't know it then. Didn't know that all these years later, I would finally understand the reason I was put on this earth. I promised you I would wait for you. I went to war for you. I worked my ass off to be there for anything you ever needed. I have strong shoulders to carry your burdens. Strong arms when you can't walk anymore. And a strong heart that loves my club and my daughter but a heart that has areas that have been locked since I took my first breath. But those areas, Doll Baby, you carved your name into them without even trying."

He took in a breath and then whispered, "I want you to know that I want everything with you. Fucking everything. And I'm here on one knee in front of you before we take that step, showing you, proving to you, that I am the man for you, Chloe. I love you, Doll Baby. Love you until the stars fall from the sky. Will you marry me?"

I didn't even try to blink back the tears, in front of me was everything I've ever wanted and then some.

Which was why I replied with, "I will love you 'til the world turns to ash."

And my man being my man, he knew my answer, stood up, wrapped me in his arms, and pulled me into his chest.

Then my lips met his in a kiss so hot I forgot where we were.

That was until he pulled back, both of us inhaling much-needed oxygen into our lungs.

He grinned, then took out the black velvet box, opened it, tagged my left hand, and slid a ring on my finger.

Only then did he let me see it.

And. Was. Perfect. Utterly perfect.

It was a vintage-style set with a huge rock.

I grinned, "Are you trying to say something with this rock?"

He winked, pressed a soft kiss on my lips, then said, "Gotta make sure those motherfuckers know that you're taken."

I grinned.

***

His hands were on my ass, and my lips were melded to his, carrying me up the stairs to his house.

Somehow, without us losing our connection, he unlocked the door.

We didn't make it past the living room.

It would seem that the only place close enough was to the couch because the moment he sat down, my lips were moving away from his lips, over his beard, and to his neck.

His lips were trailing a path along the column of my neck, and it felt so good that I had to stop what I was doing, close my eyes, and just feel.

That was until I heard something, and that was why I moaned breathily and called out, "Asher?"

His lips whispered against my neck, "Yeah, Doll Baby?"

"Your phone is ringing," I whispered.

He shrugged, "Don't give a fuck."

I moved my neck and locked my eyes with his, "But... it's probably the club."

He leaned in and nipped my chin, "Again, I don't give a fuck. Dreamt about this. With you. The entire world could be falling around us, and I wouldn't give a fuck."

Before I could open my mouth, I jumped because there was a bang, bang, bang on the front door, and then we heard, "Pres. Fucking need you."

Asher growled, carefully lifted me off his lap, and sat me down. Then I watched as he tagged his gun and then stormed to the front door, ripped it open, and pointed it at Trigger.

"Whoa. Pres. What the..." Trigger trailed off.

"Is Stella okay?" Asher asked.

Trigger nodded, "Yeah, Pres. But..."

"Is anyone on the verge of meeting the reaper?" Asher asked.

Trigger shook his head, "Nah. But..."

"Is the clubhouse on fire?" Asher asked.

Trigger, again, shook his head, "Pres. If you'd let me..."

Then in a growling low tone, he said, "Then I don't give a fuck. I'm with my woman. She fucking comes first."

I felt a tingle between my legs at his words and his tone.

Sweet baby Jesus.

Trigger held his hands up in a placating manner, "Pres. I got you. Okay. I do. But you told us that if a certain group of people ever showed back up, you wanted to be notified immediately."

I watched Asher's face.

And saw that he had locked his jaw.

This wasn't good.

Whatever it was.

Then I watched as his shoulders dropped.

At that, I called out, "Honey?"

Asher twisted his neck to look at me, his face softening.

"It's okay. I got a report I need to work on. You go handle business; I'll be here when you get done."

He bit out, "This shit isn't okay."

I could see he was struggling.

He wanted to keep the promise he made to me.

That I would always come before the club.

"Honey, it's okay. Promise. Go." I told him.

He growled, then stalked over to me, planted one fist in the back of the couch, and whispered, "We are going to continue what we started soon as I get fucking back. Okay?"

I nodded, and then I lifted my head and pressed my lips to his.

Then I watched as he walked out the door after Trigger apologized.

Three hours later, due to a gentle sway, I opened my eyes and then looked up into Asher's face.

He looked down at me and winked, "Glad you got a nap. 'Cause you're going to need it tonight."

I smiled, finally. Freaking finally.

The moment we reached his bedroom, he sat me down on my feet, keeping hold of me to ensure I was steady on my feet, then stepped to the door, closed it, and flipped the lock.

Only then did he turn back to me and said, "If you're too tired, that's fine. But Doll Baby, you want me, you fucking have me, all you have to do is say the word."

I winked, "Word."

He took in a deep breath, then moved.

And he moved by walking to me, wrapped his hands around my face, and pulled my head up for a deep, scorching kiss.

Hands moved then.

Tongues danced.

Before I knew it, he had my property patch off, and I had his kutte off, my shirt was thrown somewhere, his too.

With the feel of his chest against mine, I wanted to purr like a contented kitten.

As he kissed along the column of my neck, his hands moved to my ass, he lifted me, then walked to his bed.

Carefully, ever so carefully, he laid me down.

As his mouth and tongue did wonders, he deftly unclasped my bra, and then, well, I couldn't tell you where I ended, and he began.

My body was on fire as he worked my nipples into his mouth, the way his roughened, calloused fingers skimmed along my skin.

My pants were off, followed by my panties, and then I laid there, bared completely, while he took his feel.

I rose on my elbows and watched as he unsnapped his jeans, lowered them, and then removed his boxers, and for the first time in my entire life, I saw what a cock looked like.

I had thoughts, of course, of will it fit, it's going to break me in two, oh my word, but all those thoughts vanished when he crawled up the bed.

Then he tagged my left hand and pressed a kiss to the ring he had placed on my finger, then he whispered, "Dreamt of making love to you while this was the only thing you wore. Thank you for saying yes to me."

I smiled and whispered, "You're welcome."

My hands moved of their own accord to touch him, and my fingers trailed over his chest, and then down, until he grabbed them and whispered, "Doll baby, it's been five fucking years since I've had my dick inside another woman. Six years since my dick has seen any action other than my hand. So, I need you to be patient with me, alright?"

My breath caught. I knew Stella told me that, but hearing it from his lips, I had to clarify one thing,

"Asher, you're a biker. I thought y'all just took it and then apologized for it later?"

He winked, "Sometimes. But Doll baby, I don't apologize to a single fucking soul. But one. You."

My breath hitched.

Because I knew that wasn't a lie.

Asher didn't lie to me.

It didn't matter how much it hurt to hear the truth. But if there was one thing I knew about Asher with absolute certainty, it was that he didn't lie to me.

I lifted my head and pressed a kiss to his throat, and as my lips skinned the column of his neck, I whispered, "Thank you."

When I lowered my head, fire, passion, need, and want, blazed in those hazel eyes of his. Eyes that I wanted to melt into.

"Dad."

We both froze.

Not once did he move his eyes from me when he called out, "Yeah?"

"Can you tell Chloe that while I adore and love her, she better make you wear a condom? I've accepted this. I've pushed for this. I want you both to be happy. I do. But let me enjoy being a single child for a little bit longer. Mmkay?"

Asher's eyes twinkled, then he winked at me and said two words, "Too late."

Her gasp of indignation had both of us chuckling, "Seriously?"

Asher chuckled as he lowered his body further down the bed, pressed a kiss on my stomach, and called out, "Love you, princess. But go the fuck away."

His lips were skimming a path, lower, lower, and then I heard, "Okay. I'm going."

I giggled.

Then we both heard, "You were joking. Right?"

I almost forgot to answer her because his lips were now in an area that was on fire, his tongue twirled deliciously over my clit, and then I gasped and remembered she was still there, and she didn't need to hear me screaming her dad's name, I called out, "He's joking, Stella. But if you don't get out of this house right now, I will bleach your hair the next time you fall asleep next to me."

"Ekk. I'm out." And with that, we heard his front door slam.

As the door slammed, he hit a certain spot inside of me with his fingers, and the only thing I could do was moan out his name, "Asher."

He stopped what he was doing for a split second and whispered, "Love that."

Then he was back at it, his fingers and his tongue working a rhythm, and then, like falling off a precipice, I saw stars, lightning, and all the colors of the rainbow as I climaxed.

In a split second, Asher was on top of me, kissing me. And I didn't think I would like it, but I didn't mind the taste of me.

It was naughty, euphoric, and oh-so-good.

Then suddenly, he pulled his lips back from mine and whispered, "I could feast on your pussy for the rest of my life and never need to eat another meal for as long as I lived."

I smiled, then I felt his cock at my entrance, "I will put a condom on if you want me to, but Doll Baby, please don't ask me to do that."

I shook my head, "I'm on birth control. Have been since I made a decision that I wanted to be yours, and I wanted you to be mine."

Then he whispered, "Thank fuck."

I felt pressure, but nothing too painful, as he slowly started working his cock inside of me.

His muscles were flexing, his veins were popping, and then I watched as he gritted his teeth, froze, and then moaned, "Fuck yes."

At his moan, I felt something come over me, a want and a need so great, and it was a miracle I didn't combust there on the spot. Therefore, I whispered, "Asher, please, hurry."

His eyes stayed locked with mine as he nodded, pulled out, and then pushed back in, and as he did so, he whispered, "Keep those gorgeous eyes open, Doll Baby."

I nodded.

And then... he pulled out one more time and then said, "Take a deep breath."

I did so, and then he said, "Let it out."

And as I exhaled, he pushed all the way in.

And then he froze.

I watched as his eyes rolled back in his head for a brief second, then they were back staring into mine as he whispered, "Okay?"

I nodded, "Okay."

He grinned, then he pulled out and pushed back in, slow, delicious.

He lifted one of my legs, wrapped it around his shoulder, pulled out, and then drove back in.

He hit a spot inside of me that caused my back to bow off the bed.

"Fuck. Dreamed of this. Imagined this. But nothing. Fucking nothing could ever prepare me for the actual feel of this."

I breathed heavily, whispering, "Is that good?"

He winked, "So good that I may never leave your pussy."

And then, he thrust back in so hard, I moaned, "Again. Just like that."

To which he did. Over. And over. And over.

And then I felt my spine start to tingle, my body heated, his hand moved from the top of my thigh to my clit, and with one brush of it, I had to fight to keep my eyes open.

Another roll of his finger over my clit, and he whispered, "Give it to me, Chloe. Fuck. Please. I can't hold off any longer."

At his words, I came. And when I did, he pulled out, then slammed back in, and he, too, came.

Our breaths were mingled together, his lips were coming down to mine, and my head was lifting to meet his.

He rolled to his side, still keeping his cock buried inside of me, one of his arms went under my head, and his heavy leg was thrown over mine.

And that was how I fell asleep moments later.

His weight was on top of me, his cock still buried inside of me.

And I had the best sleep of my life.

There were so many moments I treasured with Asher.

But none of them, freaking none of them, compared to waking up in his arms, his beard skimming my bare shoulder while he whispered, "Good Morning, Doll baby."

Chapter 17

Chloe

My head was thrown back, laughing.

Asher's face had been priceless.

See, he hates tomatoes. Loathes them, to be exact.

Sometimes, he even gets green in the face if he sees anyone pick a tomato slice up and eat it.

I found a book at a bookstore yesterday.

I was one of those home remedy books.

And I had found something out.

And I had just relayed this to Asher.

He shook his head, "You mean to tell me that someone recommended ketchup as a medicine?"

I giggled, then nodded, "Yeah, apparently, in the 1830's a doctor sold tomato pills to treat things like jaundice and diarrhea."

Asher got green again, then shook his head, "I would've suffered with it."

I was still laughing when a thought suddenly occurred to me.

And I grinned.

Oh, this was going to be fun.

After our first time, I was a little embarrassed to see the spots of blood on his sheets, but he just laughed and smiled.

I took my first shower with someone else, and I adored it even more than it was Asher.

And he was right, the dang man.

I hadn't been back to my apartment except to grab clothes.

Every night, I ended my day in his bed.

He's been so gentle with me every time we make love. But while I adore it, I could tell that he was holding back.

And that crap stopped here and now.

Maybe I was biting off more than I could chew, but I knew that Asher wouldn't ever hurt me.

That was why, in the middle of the party, I ran up to our room and pulled a pair of barely their black denim ripped shorts up my legs.

Stepped to the mirror and did a bend and snap test.

Perfect.

I couldn't wait.

And I knew that I wouldn't have to wait long.

Asher

My woman disappeared.

Where the fuck did she go?

My eyes scanned the clubhouse, looking for that head of hair I loved waking up to having tossed all around me.

The euphoric feel of it as it moved across my chest.

But that feeling of euphoria dissipated when I saw her coming down the stairs and took in what she had put on.

I stormed over to her and growled, "No. I don't fucking think so. Change out of those fucking shorts."

She lifted her brow and then planted her hands on her hips.

I crowded into her, then lowered my voice, "You have one of two choices. One, I put a bullet in anyone who thinks it's okay to check out your ass. Two, you go upstairs and change, and I'm not facing consecutive life sentences for second-degree murder."

She tilted her head to the side, "Is there a third option?"

I nodded, "Yeah. I throw you over my shoulder, carry your ass upstairs, rip those shorts off your body, and then fuck you senseless. So senseless you won't be able to walk."

Her eyes glinted with a challenge, fuck, but I loved this woman, and I knew it even more so when she asked, "And you won't do that here?"

"Your body is mine. You are mine. And like fuck am I going to risk anyone seeing what's mine." I growled.

I watched as her fiery temper made itself known as she placed her hand on her hips and whispered, "I'm sorry, but what?"

I pulled her closer to my body and asked, "Are you mine?"

She narrowed her eyes but nodded.

"Am I yours?" I smiled.

She scowled, then said, "Yes, you most definitely are."

I shrugged, then, "Then... what's the problem?"

She narrowed her eyes at me, "The problem is that you've been holding back from me. I'm not going to break. Give me all of you, Asher."

I nodded, "Okay, you want it, you got it." And with that, I bent at the waist, tossed her over my shoulder, and stormed to the closest room so we wouldn't be bothered.

I had the door to the room we held church in slammed closed with my boot, and then I was dropping her to her feet.

I unsnapped her shorts and then lowered them down her legs, and made a mental note to burn the fuckers.

Then, I spun her around, pressed my hand to her back, then I kicked her legs apart.

"Grab the table, and hold the fuck on," I said as I unbuckled my belt, unsnapped my jeans, the zipper, then I was freeing my cock.

I stepped between her splayed legs, lined my cock up, and then slammed it inside of her.

And since she wanted all of me, she was going to get all of me.

The sounds of our fucking filled the room, but when I hit a spot so deep inside of her, I watched as her back bowed, and then she shouted, "Asher. Fuck. Yes."

I did it.

Or rather, my cock did it.

But I made my woman curse.

I kept pounding into her, hitting that same spot, and it wasn't long before I felt the walls of her glorious pussy clamp around my cock, and like the sucker, I was where this woman was concerned, I was following her.

After we both caught our breath, I asked, "You want a cup of hot cocoa?"

She grinned.

We got dressed, and then I tagged her hand and said, "Shorts are getting burned."

As I opened the door to church, she chuckled.

Hoots and catcalls followed us to the kitchen, and while Chloe blushed, she didn't seem embarrassed.

The moment we made it to the kitchen, I helped her up and sat her on the counter.

Then I got my woman a hot cocoa. And I poured some of those mini marshmallows on top.

After she took a few sips, she said randomly, "Just so you know, I want a big wedding."

If I knew anything like I knew the back of my hand, it was that I knew my woman, which was why I already had things in the works.

I moved in, wrapped my hand around the side of her neck, then pressed my lips to hers.

I pulled away to see her eyes still closed, and then slowly she opened them, and when she did, I whispered against her lips, "I love you, Doll Baby. Love you until the stars fall from the sky."

She whispered back, "I will love you 'til the world turns to ash."

Chapter 18

Chloe

Since I hadn't spent time at my apartment, and since Stella was getting a little weirded out by the loving we were doing, we all agreed that since Asher had paid for the apartment, Stella would move into it.

But I should have made time to talk to her.

And I mean really talk to her.

Which was why I had planned for something tonight.

Therefore, before Asher headed out to meet someone, I leaned up on my tiptoes and pressed my lips to his, then I whispered, "Will you stop by the store on your way back and grab some Hershey's chocolate for smores?"

He winked down at me, "Yes, ma'am."

"Damn, Pres. The little lady has your balls in her pocket." Stoney guffawed.

Asher grinned down at me, "Yeah, she sure fucking does."

And with that, he pressed a kiss to my nose, then headed out to his bike.

I sighed as I watched him walk through the clubhouse, almost every female's eyes watching him.

A few licked their lips, some melting visibly.

And I snickered, that man was all mine.

I didn't have a freaking thing to worry about.

After a few hours, we were all huddled around the fire pit; I had just roasted a marshmallow when I leaned in and said, "Okay, time for you to talk to me."

Stella looked at me and said, "What about?"

I ate my marshmallow, then I said, "About what's been bothering you. I'm always here, Stella."

She sighed, looked around, and said, "Can we go somewhere private?"

I looked around and then nodded.

I stood and then reached for her hand to help her up.

Then we walked into the clubhouse and to the media room.

Thankfully, since we were basically the only two who used it, it was empty.

I closed the door, flipped the lock, turned to her, and then, as I did, I watched as tears trailed down her cheeks.

My heart stuttered, my feet were moving, and thankfully, I caught her as she started to lose her footing and maneuvered her to the couch.

I was running my hand through her hair, rocking her back and forth, waiting.

Then, finally, when hiccups appeared, she whispered, "Kyrian's wife is pregnant."

I nodded, "I know. I'm so sorry, Stella."

She whimpered, "He did the same thing my dad did. He married her because she got pregnant."

I nodded. "He's a good man, Stella."

That made her cry even more.

I didn't know what to say to her.

What could I say?

That she could do better?

That would make me a hypocrite.

That she was better off without him?

Stella felt the same way about Kyrian that I did about Asher.

I wasn't sure how much time had passed until I noticed that she had cried herself to sleep.

And since half of her weight was on me, I didn't dare try to move.

Instead, I fell asleep right along with her.

Neither one of us heard the key in the lock, nor did we feel blankets being thrown over us.

And we didn't see Asher settle his big body in the chair opposite the couch and fell asleep.

All because he would be damned if he ever slept in another room without me.

***

It was finally Friday, and it was almost time to be off work.

I wasn't sure what was going on with my body, but it was off.

I honestly felt like I was coming down with the flu.

Everything hurt.

And I meant everything.

My boss even took pity on me and sent me home early.

After I grabbed my things, I got in my car and tagged my phone.

I pulled up Asher's contact and pressed dial.

His voice came through the line a few seconds later, "You okay, Doll Baby?"

He hadn't wanted me to go to work today because he knew how badly I felt.

I nodded, even though he couldn't see me, then I said, "Boss sent me home. Where are you?"

"Clubhouse. Got a few things to do. You want to come here or go home."

I wanted to wrap myself around his body and never leave it, which was why I said, "I want you."

I heard his smile in his tone, "Then come to the clubhouse, Doll Baby."

Half an hour later, I was sitting in his lap, curled into his chest, after I had taken some cold and flu medicine, he had someone go grab me.

His fingers were running through my hair, and I started thinking about what I wanted my wedding dress to look like when suddenly my thoughts were gone when I heard Stoney mutter, "What the fuck?"

I looked at him, then looked at the woman who was dragging a little girl behind her.

But what shocked me, and everyone else, was when Creature stood up, then stormed over to the woman, backhanded her so hard, she let go of the little girl, then dropped to her knees.

And even more, what shocked me and everyone else was when Creature knelt in front of the little girl, wiped her tears off her cheeks, and rumbled out through his messed up vocal cords, "What's wrong Shortcake?"

The little girl sniffled, then said, "I tripped. Ripped my new dress. Mommy got mad at me. My knee hurts, Creat."

My jaw dropped when Creature nodded, then lifted the girl in his arms, turned his head and looked at Ox, and said, "You end that bitch, or else I will."

And with that, Creature walked into the clubhouse with the little girl in his arms, her face pressed into his neck.

I jerked my head and looked at Asher, "Who was that?"

He looked down at me and lowered his tone, "Ox's on again, off again, fling. He tried to end it with her, but she got pregnant. Brenda is a bitch. That little girl is Natalie."

I shook my head, "How come I've never met either of them before?"

"Because Brenda refuses to come here to get back at Ox. Like I said, off-again, on-again type of shit."

After all of that, the medicine kicked in, and I fell asleep.

It wasn't until hours later when we were getting in line to make our plates, that I heard Asher roar, "What the fuck?" as he shoved me behind him while cops poured into the clubhouse.

My eyes flew in every direction, trying to take everything in that was happening.

But what shocked me even more was when Creature stood up, then walked to the cops, turned, and put his hands behind his back, then looked at Asher.

"You keep her safe. She's mine."

Asher's body was tense beneath my fingertips.

But I watched as Asher nodded.

We all knew who Creature was referring to.

Thankfully, Natalie wasn't here to see any of this.

It wasn't until the lawyer that the club used relayed what had happened.

Apparently, Brenda had been beating on Natalie. And Ox refused to do anything about it.

So, alongside Brenda, went Ox into a shallow grave.

The club had few laws.

But hurting kids was one of the biggest.

One week later, we sat in that courtroom as Creature was sentenced to twenty-five years without the possibility of parole for killing two people.

Chapter 19

Asher

Two weeks later, as we were dancing in the middle of the clubhouse, I asked, "Need you to clarify something for me, okay?"

She looked up at me and nodded, "Okay, what?"

"That day when we had the party, and you called me Pres. What the fuck was wrong?" I asked her and then watched as her cheeks turned pink.

She tried to hide her face from me by burying it in my chest, but I decided that wasn't going to work for me, which was why I moved my hand from her back and lifted her chin.

"Tell me," I whispered

She sighed, "I had a dream about you."

I lifted a brow, "Oh, what was I doing in this dream?"

"You were going down on me, then you were kissing me, telling me you loved me, then right as you were going to put your cock inside of me, my alarm went off. And I was embarrassed."

"So that's what was going on that night I sat outside your house," I told her.

She gasped, "Wait, you were there that night?"

I nodded, "I was."

One delicate brow lifted, "Why?"

"Couldn't sleep. And I had a feeling. Needed to be there in case some dumb motherfucker thought it was okay to climb through your window."

That was when she chuckled, "And what's your excuse for now? Seeing as you didn't think it was a good idea to sleep with the bedroom window open."

I winked down at her, "You got me now. Any motherfucker who is dumb enough to try to break into this house, he'll be one less dumb motherfucker of this world."

She threw her head back and laughed.

Just then, as I reveled in the sound of her laughter, I caught Trigger, who jerked up his chin.

Then the chords to our song started playing, and with my entire world in my arms, I lowered my head and sang to her.

Tears that had been glistening in her eyes slowly began to trickle down her cheeks.

With that soft smile of hers, I would start wars over and not blink an eye.

***

We were out looking at wedding dresses, and she kept secretly caressing my dick.

"Behave," I whispered as I tugged at her lobe with my teeth.

She smiled, "Now, where's the fun in that?"

And with that, she took a picture of us in the window we had just passed.

"Freaking amazing." She said as she stared at it.

I grinned, "Yeah, you."

I crowded into her space, my hand going to the side of her neck, my other hand wrapping around her body, pulling her close to me.

Staring down into her eyes as she stared up into mine.

The moment was so profound that neither one of us paid attention to the woman who had stopped and stared at us.

Both of us were in our own little world.

"I love you, Chloe."

She smiled, "I love you too, Asher."

"Well, now I see why you never texted me back and blocked me. You like it younger. Do I need to go have surgery performed and reattached my hymen."

I didn't give the bitch a moment of my time, and neither did Chloe.

She winked up at me, tagged my hand, and then pulled me right along with her.

And just like that, I was powerless.

She held all the power, and it would be a cold day in hell before I ever denied it.

After the last place we visited, when she would let me see the dress she chose, we ended up at the clubhouse.

She was at the bar ordering a drink, and I had seen a hint of that thong when her shirt rose, showing everyone and their brother that perfect skin on her lower back.

That just wouldn't do.

Therefore, I got up, stalked over to her, crowded into her back, leaned in, and whispered against her neck, "Tell me."

The scent of buttercream, vanilla, and strawberries wafted up through my senses.

Her voice was husky when she whispered, "Tell you what?"

I smiled against her skin, "Oh, is that how you want to play this?"

She shrugged, "I have no clue what you're talking about."

I chuckled, "Is that right? So, you mean I didn't see you slip on my favorite color over your perfect little pussy?"

I felt her shiver against me.

"You'll just have to wait and see," she said as she winked.

I growled until I heard, "Uh, Pres?"

I winked at Chloe and then looked at Trigger, "Yeah?"

"Think you and Chloe should go take care of that problem you have. Having a hard-on on the bike ain't too comfortable."

Chloe threw her head back and laughed, when she stopped, her eyes were twinkling, "Told you not to get worked up."

I shrugged. "A little pain on the bike over making sure my woman knows how I feel. Give me all the pain."

She giggled, then carried her drink to the table.

I pressed a kiss to her lips and then headed out to my bike with my brothers, thinking of everything I could to get my dick to go down.

Which had me cursing the fucker, and the brothers who were riding with me laughing their asses off.

I had just caught sight of Pagan finishing his sandwich, and when he opened his mouth, and I saw that food there, yeah, that did it.

Chloe

And yes, my man gave me my whole wedding.

Everything I could have ever dreamed of and more.

Then the moment happened.

The two prospects the club had voted on opened the white fabric and revealed me on my father's arm.

That was when I saw him.

I saw my forever.

The man I've wanted the entire time I've been on this earth.

And I couldn't wait to live the rest of my life forever with him.

My father looked down at me, and I looked up at him, then he lowered his head and whispered, "He might be a bad son of a bitch. But if he's any man at all, he's going to shed a tear or two when you walk toward him. He doesn't, I'll kick his ass."

I snickered, then whispered back, "I'd have all my money on you."

Then, as the wedding march started, we headed up the aisle.

And my father was right. I smiled as I watched my big badass president of a one percent motorcycle club bring his hand up and wipe away a tear... or two from his eyes.

"Damn, I can't kick his ass."

I smiled, and then I winked at Asher.

My love. My life.

Once Powers announced, I now pronounce you as Mr. and Mrs. Asher Samuel Hendrix's, my husband wrapped an arm around my waist and dipped me backward, I wrapped my hand around his bicep and pressed my lips to his.

It was perfect. Utterly perfect.

His tongue tangled with mine in a heated passion.

When he pulled his lips away, I winked, and then I said, "So, I hope you're ready for dirty diapers."

He froze in helping me back up.

And I hoped, like all get out, that the photographer Asher had hired.

Then I watched as my husband smiled, huge.

However, somehow, in the blink of an eye, I was up in his arms.

My arms went around his shoulders, my face pressed into his neck, and when he shouted, "My wife is making me a dad again. Fuck yes."

Everyone gasped, then clapped, and I giggled.

There, in the middle of the back courtyard, as our song played over the speakers, I sang to my husband, *"I will work for you 'til my hands are tired and bleedin'. I know what it is from us I'm needin'; I will work for you."*

Then, I watched a tear fall from the corner of his eye. I grinned, reached my hand up, and wiped the tear away, and then I licked it off my thumb.

And I also finally found out the meaning behind the necklace he had given me on my eighteenth birthday. It was to tell me, even back then, that I was his light in the darkness, his calm in a storm.

That night, he caressed my belly after he made slow, sweet love to me.

And I fell asleep to my husband singing our song to our babies, who were currently the size of raspberries.

Asher

The past seven months have been nothing short of a whirlwind.

Chloe had me gagging for her body every minute of every day. There was nothing more beautiful than seeing her with my child nestled in her body.

Chloe had finally given in and told me what was wrong with Stella, and it killed me, but there was nothing I could do for her.

And that broke my heart.

I couldn't fix it. Well, I could.

I could kill the bitch Kyrian was married to, make sure his kid stayed safe, and then kidnap Kyrian.

Hmmm....

***

Chloe was asleep in our bed at the clubhouse, and this run had to happen.

We needed to help a woman and her three kids escape a polygamy situation.

I was strapping what I needed on my bike when Whit walked over and said, "You going to tell Chloe?"

I shook my head, "Nah, tell her after. She doesn't need the stress right now."

Whit shared a look with Pipe, Coal, Irish, Stoney, Rome, Gravel, and Hippie.

Then, they all either shook their heads or chuckled.

But it was Stoney who muttered, "You're fucking up, boyo. But I am all here for the fireworks. And the ass-kicking she's about to give you."

I scoffed, "My woman loves me. She's not going to kick my ass."

Famous last words.

I really should have heeded their advice.

I really fucking should have.

Because seven hours later, after we all got shot at by the dumbass son of a bitch, we dropped the woman and her three kids off with Powers at the Mississippi state line, so they could go to their next destination when we pulled into the clubhouse.

As I dismounted from my bike, it was to see my woman with her arms crossed over her pregnant belly, tapping her foot.

"You motherfucking lying piece of shit," she screamed at me.

I held my hands up, "Doll Baby, let me..."

She snarled, "Go to hell, Asher. I woke up, and you were nowhere to be freaking found. Nowhere. I needed help getting out of bed. In case you missed the memo, I'm as big as a flipping house."

She took in a breath and continued before I could get a word out, "You promised me that I came first. That me and your kiddos came first. You're lucky that I was able to finagle my way off the bed before I peed myself. And just for that, your butt is on the couch tonight."

"Doll Baby, I know, and I'm sorry. It was time sensitive." I told her, and it was.

Her eyes flashed, and immediately, I knew that was the wrong thing to say.

She growled, "Time sensitive?" her chest was rising and falling rapidly, "Time. Sensitive? It was time-sensitive over an hour ago when we were supposed to be at our doctor's appointment to make sure the twins were in the proper placement for delivery. It was time-sensitive for us to be there so we could ensure they were healthy. It was time sensitive for us to go over our birth plan."

Fuck.

Me.

I ran my hand through my hair and muttered, "Shit."

The brother's eyes were on me, and I knew they were all smirking.

Stoney piped up then, "We tried to warn him, mama. He didn't think you would be mad."

She glared, "Then y'all should have forced him to postpone this time-sensitive matter for four hours. You all knew that we had an appointment today. It was written on the freaking calendar so y'all wouldn't be interrupting him on important matters. Are y'all trying to tell me that the birth of our daughters isn't important?"

None of them spoke.

Chloe growled, then stomped into the clubhouse.

Knowing her mood, I hauled my ass after her.

My brothers followed suit.

When the door opened, it was for everyone to hear, "If you're not a brother, get the fuck out of this clubhouse. If you're a club girl, enjoy your freaking night off and go have some fun. Consequences be damned."

Fuck.

Shit.

Pres.

"Chloe, Darlin', don't be like that," Trigger held his hands up.

Chloe spun on her heel, her arms crossed over her very pregnant belly, and she lifted a brow. "If Mama isn't happy. Then nobody is happy. Get the fuck over it."

Yeah, she was pissed.

She was madder than hell.

Her temper showed it.

Her decisions showed it.

But it was the curse word that fell from her lips that told that truth.

Slowly, with my hands up, I walked to her and then carefully wrapped her in my arms.

"I'm so sorry, Doll Baby. But there was a woman who was being beaten, and she already miscarried three kids. She couldn't go through anymore. And she needed to be here for the three kids she already had. We had one opportunity to get them out. I'm sorry. I love you."

She huffed, then said, "I love you too, you inconsiderate jackass. Your ass is still on the couch tonight."

And with that, she moved away from me and left the clubhouse.

Trigger asked in a low tone, "Since she's gone, think we can call the club girls back?"

But apparently, it wasn't low enough for my woman not to hear it, "If you call the club girls back here, every single one of you will also be caught off from Kitty Korner for a freaking week. Don't. Test. Me."

Every single one of the brothers winced.

Which was why I asked, "Why didn't y'all try harder?"

And yes, that night, I slept on the fucking couch.

My daughter walked out of my house snickering.

But thankfully, my woman didn't sleep that well if I wasn't in bed next to her.

And yes, to show how very sorry I was, I gave her a back massage and a foot massage.

She was asleep for all of three hours when she woke me up.

And two hours later, she was hooked up to monitors.

My woman told every single person we encountered, "When you're ready to pop, but the babies are being stubborn, get a back and foot massage from your man. It works wonders."

Epilogue

Chloe

Our twin daughters were now six months old, and I loved them to pieces.

Staring at them made the whole birth experience that much better.

Sure, it was painful, but they were worth it.

It was worth it even more to stand here leaning against the doorway to their nursery while my husband sang our song to our daughters.

Juniper Marie Hendrix weighed five pounds and nine ounces.

Melodie Julia Hendrix weighed five pounds and seven ounces.

They both had my dark hair, my eyes, and my nose, and they were mini replicas of me.

And my husband boasted about that every chance he had.

He also cursed them for all they were worth any time someone told him he needed to buy more shotguns.

***

One of the things about Asher's house I had changed... that was making the nook that overlooked the driveway into a reading corner.

And yes, I got my purple wingback chair to read in and still laughed at the memory of the first time Stella had laid her eyes on it.

In addition to that little reading corner, on the end table, were two candlestick holders. One of them was the very same one I had used to hit Marco with.

Asher told me that in case there was ever a fire, the candlestick holder better be one of the things we saved.

Also, I had found Asher's stash of all the *Reese Cups* I had given him. We had tossed the chocolate and peanut butter concoction and saved the wrappers.

They were now all together in a memory box hanging in the hallway that led to our bedroom.

Five Years Later

"Is your man card going to be revoked?" I teased.

He looked down at me, then at our two girls, and shook his head, "Nah, the only way my man card gets revoked is if I don't sit there and watch the whole movie with a smile on my face."

And that was how Asher, the president of Zagan MC, the club that dominated the entire state of Mississippi, got looks as he led our twin daughters through the theater and to the room that was playing Barbie.

And underneath his kutte was a bright pink shirt with the word Barbie in bright white letters.

Damn, but I loved this man.

Loved him with everything in me.

But the reason I loved him even more?

That was because the moment we walked up the stairs, and in the three rows at the back sat every single member of Zagan MC. All were wearing the same shirt as Asher.

And yes, even Rome, but we were missing one person... Creature.

In the next letter, I wrote to him... I would just have to tell him all about this night.

I knew he wouldn't laugh... but... I had a feeling that some information about a certain young lady might make him smile.

Maybe.

***

Things over the past five years haven't changed too much.

Hanna and Kayla were still club girls.

Sutton owned Irish's heart, and their girl Maisie was a force to be reckoned with.

Flo... well... she left, however, what none of us realized, and something we definitely should have was that Flo wasn't going to go after any of the taken members.

No, she was going after one member in particular.

And god help her because this time, she had bitten off more than she could chew.

And she did that by going after the one being that has owned Creature's heart.

Another woman vying for a brother's heart was Leighton. The same woman who had tried her best to help me in that diner on that fateful day.

Rome... well... he was still a brother of the club, but he was technically a nomad. Because his woman was at a college in another MC's territory.

As for Stella... well... she had needed a break after Kyrian's wife, being the epic bitch she was, took her son to Stella so she could cut his hair.

She had gone to visit another club.

And... well... she did what most women would do.

She got underneath another man in hopes of getting over Kyrian.

Asher

Two Years Later

I had half a mind to dig up that fucker's grave and beat the shit out of him.

However, the moment I held that little bundle in my arms and saw the tired smile on my daughter's face, I knew I wouldn't do it.

Because it would upset her.

And there was nothing I would ever do that would cause her to be upset.

It had ripped my heart out when my baby girl, my firstborn born, had gotten the call that the father of her baby had been gunned down in a drive-by shooting from a rival club.

Unfortunately, that also meant not kicking the fucker who just randomly showed up in her hospital room.

His bitch of a wife at his side and their handsome son.

Two Years Later

I was leaning against the island while flour and god knew what covered my woman and my two girls, along with Stella and her little girl Ivy.

Laughing my ass off as I thought about how hard it was going to be to get all of that junk out of their hair.

Chloe was laughing as she sidled up next to me, and I didn't hesitate to wrap my arm around her waist and pull her into my body.

She grinned up at me, "Are you sure?"

I lifted a brow, "Am I sure about what, Doll Baby?"

She smiled, "That you don't want to try for a son?"

I shook my head. "Nah. Meant to be a girl dad. And that's alright with me. They will be the most kickass kids ever created. I can tell you that right now."

***

"If I could do it, I'd fucking live in your pussy, Doll Baby," I said as I slid out of my wife, undulated my hips, and then slid back in.

She grinned, winked, then whispered, "If it were possible, I'd let you."

"Wanna make another baby?" I asked her as I pulled out and then slammed into her hard.

Her gasp, followed by her moan... I fucking lived for those moans of hers.

When I did it again, and then again, and then again, I knew she forgot what I had asked her.

Her nails were digging into my back, and I would wear those claiming marks with my chest puffed out with pride.

This woman undid me.

I wasn't the president of a one percent motorcycle club to her.

I was simply her husband.

Her confidant.

Her second-best friend.

Her protector.

The father of her children.

And until the day I died, those were the only titles I would die to keep.

After we were through, I came three times, and my woman came seven times, her little body was curled into mine.

Her breaths flowed over my skin, and then she whispered, "Last time I was in labor, you told me we were never doing this again because your heart couldn't take it. I guess that's changed?"

I sighed, "Fuck. Yeah, no. Find a way for me to carry the baby, and we will have another one."

She giggled, "It doesn't work like that."

"I can guaran-damn-tee that any man who loves his woman wishes it could happen. Felt like someone had grabbed my heart and ripped it from my chest every time you cried out in pain."

With the softest of kisses, she pressed one over my heart, snuggled into my side, and whispered, "God couldn't have created a better man for me had he tried."

"I'm going to love you until the stars fall from the sky," I whispered as I pressed a kiss atop her head.

And we fell asleep like that.

Holding onto each other as tight as we could.

That was until she rolled away from me, and even in my sleep, that wasn't acceptable.

The End.

Thank You

Thank you from the bottom of my heart for reading Asher and Chloe's book.

I know it's different from what I usually do, but I hope I did their story justice.

As always, again, thank you!!!

I hope you loved it.

And it you needed to cry, I was able to give you that.

If you needed to curse someone out, I was able to give you that.

And if you needed an escape, I provided you with that.

Stalk Me

Website

https://tiffanycasper.net

Facebook

https://www.facebook.com/author.tiffany.casper

Instagram

https://www.instagram.com/authortiffanycasper/

Goodreads

https://www.goodreads.com/author/show/19027352.Tiffany_Casper

Other Works

Wrath MC

Mountain of Clearwater

Clearwater's Savior

Clearwater's Hope

Clearwater's Fire

Clearwater's Miracle

Clearwater's Treasure

Clearwater's Luck

Clearwater's Redemption

Christmas in Clearwater

Dogwood's Treasure

Dove's Life

Phoenix's Plight

Raven's Climb

Wren's Salvation

Lo's Wraith

Sparrow's Grace

Lark's Precious

DeLuca Empire

The Devil & The Siren

The Cleaner & The Princess

The Soldier & The Dancer

As If...

Cold As Ice

Dark As Coal

Smooth As Whiskey

Zagan MC

Asher

Willow Creek

Where Hearts Align

Pinewood Lake

Rise

Empower

Charlotte U

Perfectly Imperfect

Imperfection is Beauty

Virgin Mary's

Old-Fashioned

Novella's

Hotter Than Sin

Silver Treasure

Wrath Ink

Made in the USA
Middletown, DE
18 February 2025

71193207R00184